INTRODUCING
BENJAMIN TAMMUZ

NAL takes great pleasure in introducing Israeli novelist Benjamin Tammuz to American readers. MINOTAUR, brilliantly translated from the Hebrew and hailed as a literary masterpiece, is both a startling love story and a taut thriller that draws us into the shadow-filled world of passion and betrayal. Because NAL believes deeply in the extraordinary talent of Mr. Tammuz, and wants his work to become widely known in the United States, MINOTAUR is being offered at an unusually modest price to make it accessible to readers of fine fiction everywhere.

At the close of this book, readers will find a selection from Benjamin Tammuz's REQUIEM FOR NA'AMAN, a superbly written novel of a family, a people, and a nation through four generations—presently available in an NAL Books hardcover edition.

Sensational SIGNET Bestsellers

- [ ] **BRAIN by Robin Cook.** (#AE1260—$3.95)
- [ ] **THE DELTA DECISION by Wibur Smith.** (#AE1335—$3.50)
- [ ] **CENTURY by Fred Mustard Stewart.** (#AE1407—$3.95)
- [ ] **ORIGINAL SINS by Lisa Alther.** (#AE1448—$3.95)
- [ ] **MAURA'S DREAM by Joel Gross.** (#AE1262—$3.50)
- [ ] **THE DONORS by Leslie Alan Horvitz and H. Harris Gerhard, M.D.** (#AE1338—$2.95)
- [ ] **SMALL WORLD by Tabitha King.** (#AE1408—$3.50)
- [ ] **THE KISSING GATE by Pamela Haines.** (#AE1449—$3.50)
- [ ] **THE CROOKED CROSS by Barth Jules Sussman.** (#AE1203—$2.95)
- [ ] **CITY KID by Mary MacCracken.** (#AE1336—$2.95)
- [ ] **CHARLIES DAUGHTER by Susan Child.** (#AE1409—$2.50)
- [ ] **JUDGMENT DAY by Nick Sharman.** (#AE1450—$2.95)
- [ ] **THE DISTANT SHORE by Susannah James.** (#AE1264—$2.95)
- [ ] **FORGED IN BLOOD (Americans at War #2) by Robert Leckie.** (#AE1337—$2.95)
- [ ] **TECUMSEH by Paul Lederer.** (#AE1410—$2.95)
- [ ] **THE JASMINE VEIL by Gimone Hall.** (#AE1451—$2.95)*

*Prices Slightly Higher in Canada

Minotaur

BY BENJAMIN TAMMUZ

*Translated by Kim Parfitt
and Mildred Budny*

Ⓞ
A SIGNET BOOK
NEW AMERICAN LIBRARY
TIMES MIRROR

CHAPTER ONE

Secret Agent

1.

A man, who was a secret agent, parked his hired car in a rain-drenched square, and took a bus into town.

That day he had turned forty-one, and as he dropped into the first seat he came across, he closed his eyes and fell into bleak contemplation of his birthday. The bus pulled up at the next stop, jerking him back to consciousness, and he saw two girls sitting down on the empty seat in front of him. The girl on the left had hair the color of copper—dark copper with a glint of gold. It was sleek and gathered at the nape of her neck with a black velvet ribbon, tied in a cross-shaped bow. This ribbon, like her hair, radiated a crisp freshness, a pristine freshness to be found in things as yet untouched by a fingering hand. Whoever tied that ribbon with such meticulous care? wondered the man of forty-one. Then he waited for the moment when she would turn her profile to her friend, and when she turned to her friend and he saw her features, his mouth fell open in a stifled cry. Or did it perhaps escape from his mouth? Anyway, the passengers did not react.

2.

Today I'm forty-one and this is not the first time I've celebrated my birthday filling in a diary in a hotel room.

Tomorrow I'll find a greetings telegram at the embassy from my wife and the two girls. And there'll be a special telegram from my son at boarding school. He is also away from home, and if he likes it that way, no doubt he'll follow in my footsteps. If he does, there'll be another reason for me to end it all as soon as possible. Except that early this evening it finally happened, and now I want to hang on.

I don't know why I believed that before meeting her I would receive some sort of advance notice. At any rate, it never occurred to me that I might be taken by surprise. But I was. I saw her quite suddenly, sitting down in front of me on the bus. I had no difficulty whatsoever in recognizing her. When she got off the bus I followed her. I already have found out her address and tomorrow I shall also know her surname and possibly even her Christian name. She lives in a smart building, the sort occupied by the well-off. I heard her speaking to her friend and even her voice gave her away. She might well sing in a choir. Her accent bears witness to a good education; her clothes are simple but expensive. Not a single ornament, apart from a black velvet ribbon: a somber ribbon tied with a marvelous precision that gave the desired impression—carelessness. The color of her hair is just as I remembered it, and so is the color of her eyes—a deep brown, not too dark. Her chin juts out a little, just far enough to leave no doubts about the kind of person she is: of sufficient character to dismiss anything unwanted but, above all, capable of wholehearted and passionate devotion. Her coloring and complexion are as I remembered them: very fair, like my mother's, with a pink bloom deepening, flawless and unhurried, toward high cheekbones, so gradually that it is impossible to say where white turns into pink. But her mouth is a sudden, vivid crimson. And those teeth. My God! Surely they cannot have been created just to chew food. If they were, I'd say that there was no need to go to so much trouble.

And I am forty-one and she is about seventeen. Twenty-four years.

4

3.

Thea,

This letter, which is typewritten, is not signed and I daresay we shall never meet. Yet I have seen you and I made sure that you saw me. That was about six weeks ago. I walked past you and you looked at me, the way you look at people coming toward you in the street. You didn't recognize me. But even so, you belong to me.

You will never have an opportunity to ask me questions, but my voice will reach you through my letters, and I know that you will read them. How do I know? I can offer no explanation, other than what I am about to tell you: For as long as I can remember I have been searching for you. I knew that you existed, but I didn't know where. My work brought me to the town where you live. My work is a series of surmises, assumptions, and risks. I chose this work because I have never loved anyone, except you, although all my life I have been trying to love—in other words, to be unfaithful to you. I have devoted my life to tough and disagreeable work because I needed to love. And therefore I love the country I serve, her mountains, her valleys, her dust and despair, her roads and her paths. I acted as I did through lack of choice. I didn't know if I would ever meet you. And now, now that we have met, it's too late. There has been a mistake, some sort of discrepancy in birth dates, in passports. Even heaven is chaotic, just like any other office. Anyway, it's too late and it's quite impossible.

I have the address of your boarding school and I also know which university you will be attending next year. And I know that you like music. In due course I shall know still more.

With this letter there will be a parcel, containing a record player and a record. I'd like you to play the record next Sunday at 1700 hours. I shall do the same in my room in the hotel, not far from you, and the two of us will be listening to the same music at the very same

5

time. This will be our first meeting, and I shall know if you have done as I asked. Indeed, I already know that you will respond to this appeal.

I love you. I have loved you all my life. It is difficult for me to come to terms with the thought that you did not recognize me in the street. But that's not your fault. There has been a mistake: in dates, in places, in everything. I'm quite sure that it was me who was intended to be tormented, not you.

I take your shoe off your foot and kiss your toes. I know them, just as I know every line of your body. Don't be angry, don't take pity. I never knew happiness until I found you.

4.

Funny Man!

I did as you asked at 1700 hours precisely. How did you know that I am playing this concerto right now? For that matter, how do you come to know so much about everything? I've been trying to guess who you are and I think that I have it. If I am right you'll have to give in and come out into the open. It is true that you are G.R., and that we met at a party at N.'s? You were looking at me all the time and they told me your name.

I don't have anywhere to send this letter, but I'm writing it so that I can show it to you if we ever meet. I'm writing because it's impolite not to answer a letter as nice as yours. (By the way, I hardly understood a word of it. You're awfully mysterious.) Meanwhile I'm putting my reply in a special box, marked "Letters to Mr. Anonymous," until we meet. It's not nice to keep a girl in suspense like this.

Yours,
Thea

5.

My anonymous friend,

I think you should know that I have exams soon and I can't answer every single one of your letters, especially when you write every day and sometimes twice a day. I'm writing a general answer to all the letters that have come so far and, until the exams are over, I shan't write anymore, and you will just have to forgive me.

Now I am sure that you are not G.R., because in the meantime he has introduced himself to me and performed all sorts of amorous maneuvers. And so you remain unidentified and I am angry because your letters are becoming so sad and I'd like to tell you that there is no need to take me so seriously. Of late I've been looking in the mirror a lot, to find out what you see in me, and do you know what I discovered? I should be ashamed of myself, but it's true. I discovered that maybe I really am prettier than I thought. And this is all your fault. Now it's difficult for me to enjoy the compliments I get from my friends because, compared to your letters, everything they say sounds crude. Although I don't know you, I am sure that you are cleverer than all my friends, but I sometimes think that you exaggerate terribly. And why are you so sad? If you wanted, you could be a writer or a poet, even if you don't mean what you write.

And why do you talk about wanting to die? If you love me, as you say in all your letters, you simply have to show your face. Perhaps I'll like you? Why all this bizarre mystery? You seem to explain everything, but I understand nothing. I'm not as bright as you think.

And thanks a lot for the other two records you sent. You seem to be crazy about this one composer, as you're always sending me his music. I agree that he is wonderful, and I play the records on Sundays at 1700 hours. All according to your madness. As you can see,

I'm behaving like a good girl and it's about time that you were a good boy too and sent me a photo at least.

Your friend,
Thea

P.S. This letter is going into the "Letters to Mr. Anonymous" box too. How much longer will you be anonymous?

6.

Dearest Mr. Anonymous,

I have finished with exams and now I shall sit about listening to the records that have been piling up. Did you know that you are very impolite? This is the third letter I have written to you in the past year and I still have no address to send them to.

I know no more about you today than I did after receiving your first letter. But there is a big difference: If you were to stop writing to me now, I should miss you. Perhaps that's your intention? You make me feel like a queen and I'm getting used to it. Where will it all end? No one but you knows all the fine qualities you see in me. You are making me grow accustomed to something no one else will ever give me. Why are you doing it? I shan't write to you anymore unless you come and introduce yourself. This is the last letter I'm putting in the "Letters to Mr. Anonymous" box. Now I'm going to play a record and I hope that you will be playing one at the same time. Then you will understand that I want to see you, without any obligation, of course. In spite of everything you're still a dear.

Your friend,
Thea

7.

Thea,

I must beg your forgiveness for the contents of the last two letters. I had no right to involve you in my weeping and wailing. I am ashamed of myself and promise never to do such a thing again.

I dreamed about you last night. I was standing alone on a balcony and you appeared in the doorway, looked at me, and smiled. Then you came toward me. You didn't really walk but floated through the air to stand by my side. You neither embraced me nor reached out to me but leaned slightly toward me and kissed me on the lips; I burst into tears, and you smiled and said, "I belong to you. Take me." I said, "How can I take you?" And you said, "In the air. Take me in the air."

What did you mean, Thea? Two weeks ago I saw the graduation ceremony at your school. I was sitting on the third row, on the right, not far from your parents. When you looked at them your eyes rested momentarily on my face. Thank you, my love. I kissed you in the air, just as you suggested in my dream. You didn't recognize me. Yet again you didn't recognize me.

I shall be in town in a few months' time. I shall not go to your university, because there it would be easy to pick out a stranger. On that wretched campus you will be lost to me for a long time. I'll try to see you during vacations when you come home for a holiday. I know you will not be angry about all this absurd mystery that surrounds me. It's not a mystery at all. There is simply no other way. There is not, believe me.

I love you.

8.

Thea,

It is three years today since I found you. You are my greatest loss, a loss that was recovered only when it was already too late. Only today did it occur to me that you might perhaps like to write to me once. So this is what I suggest you do: Write on the envelope "Mr. Franz Kafka, Poste Restante," and send it to your local post office. I shall be there on December 5. At 1700 hours I shall go to the post office to collect your letter. In order to be sure that you don't come to identify me, I would like you to sit in the café opposite your parents' home at that time. One of my friends will go there to confirm that you are doing as I ask. He will phone me and then I shall go to the post office and collect your letter. If you are not in the café I shall not go to the post office. Forgive me if my suspicions are groundless.

9.

Thea,

The girl you sent to the post office to identify me did not see me but one of my friends. In the post office we saw a girl keeping a lookout and I realized that you were trying to outwit me. You have no idea how grateful I am for the fact that you wanted to see me and that you went to so much trouble. Even in my misfortune I am the happiest man in the world.

I have read your letters. You are as kind as I expected, you are as lovely as I know you to be, you are not my mistake, Thea. In my work I must never misjudge people's characters, because if I were to make a mistake even once, I might have to pay for it with my life. If I had been wrong about you I should have been dead a long time ago.

I want to answer all your questions but I cannot answer them in the way that you suggest. What I do have to say is this: I know that besides the things that we can readily understand, examine, analyze, and make use of, there is within us—and perhaps also outside us—a conscious force infinitely wiser than the intellect at our disposal. I collaborate with this force every day, especially in my work. And if I am still alive, it means that this force is not an illusion. It is likely to bring about my downfall, I suppose, but it's the best guide I have, the one that has shown you to me for as long as I remember. And it is a fact that you really do exist, exactly as I knew you before I found you. I need no better proof than this.

At the same time something has gone wrong, a mistake or a deliberate punishment. At any rate, we can't be what we were meant to be. We can't meet and we can't be united. The reason for this is simple, mundane, and humiliating, but I don't want to spell it out, because if I do, you will know that I am afraid and then you will doubt my love. There, I have already said too much.

I love you, Thea. If there is a God, he will make us meet in the place where I first divined or dreamed of you, before you were born. If he will not make this gesture on our behalf, it means that he is not God, or that he does not exist, or that he is nothing but an office—efficient but indifferent.

You exist and every day I kiss your fingers and your toes. Soon I shall dare to touch your cheeks. I shall do it first with my hand and then with my lips. I hope to dream of you tonight.

10.

About four years after the secret agent met Thea, G.R. asked her to marry him. Her parents gave their consent and the wedding was arranged for the beginning of winter.

About a month before the wedding G.R. was killed in a car crash. The same week Thea submitted her final dissertation to the university. Shortly after the death of her fiancé she went to Gstaad with her parents, and when they reached the hotel, she found a bouquet of roses waiting for her and a box of chocolates with a letter.

Thea,

God wants you to be happy so you must get over this. You will find peace of mind in your walks around the district. You are young and intelligent. There can be no doubt that you will get over it.

I have no right to bother you with words now, and I certainly have no right to set you any unnecessary riddles, and so I shall say only this, in order to put your mind at rest. You will be wondering about the bouquet that was waiting for you at the hotel. Well, it's quite simple. I learn about your actions, your movements, and your plans from various people around you. I pay them for their trouble. And to make things even simpler, I shall give you an example. In the café opposite your house there used to be an old waiter. He has since died, so I am not afraid to reveal his identity. He used to receive regular payments in exchange for the reports he gave me on whatever he managed to find out. People like that are to be found everywhere and people like myself do not hesitate to make use of their services.

Don't be angry, it's the only way open to me. I travel a lot and I am not a permanent resident in your country. If I had relied on chance alone, I would have lost you long ago. I am satisfied with what chance gave me when I found you.

Please smile, my angel. Smile, even in your grief, at me, at yourself, and at all that's terrible and wonderful in our lot.

P.S. Next Sunday I shall be in the district. If you need anything or if you want to write to me, leave your letter at the post office and at 1700 hours I shall go and collect it. You are to sit in the café below the hotel. Our usual arrangement.

11.

My anonymous friend, my only friend at this time,

Thank you for the flowers and the chocolates. I told my parents that they were from friends at the university. There, because of you I lied to them, and not for the first time. No one in the world would ever understand what there is between us. I don't really understand it myself, but do I have any choice?

The tragic death of G.R. was seven times worse because I saw it as divine retribution. I don't understand why G.R. was punished and not I, because I had sinned against him and not he against me. I was about to marry him without being really in love with him. I was very fond of him as I told you in my letters, but my love for him was not deep enough to justify marriage. This God that you call an office, for some reason, probably got the wrong address. Why did poor G.R. have to give his life to prevent the wrong I was about to do him? My anonymous friend, I am not as wonderful as you make me out to be. Now you see that I am small and pitiable and even ugly. What do I have to smile about? I wrote my final dissertation on Luis de Góngora, as you know, and when I saw G.R. pale and dead I thought,

Un cuerpo con poca sangre
Pero con dos corazones,*

and at the same time I told myself quite shamelessly that it was not about G.R. that de Góngora wrote this marvelous verse. If I thought that G.R. had had two hearts, I might have loved him with all of my one.

I am writing this letter in the café where I shall be sitting on Sunday at 1700 hours and I am amusing myself with the thought that you might be here now, among the dozens of people in the room, or that you are outside looking in at me through the window. Look how you dominate me, my anonymous friend. You are cruel

---

* A body with little blood/But with two hearts.

when all's said and done, and the worst of it is that I
don't believe you and I still think that we shall meet in
the end. If I am disappointed in you I shall never forgive you.

12.

When Thea was hired to teach Spanish literature in a
provincial university in the south, her anonymous friend
already knew enough Spanish to introduce a few Spanish
sentences into his letters. On his travels he had a diction-
ary with him in his pocket, so that he would not make spell-
ing mistakes.

Ay, Thea, lejana y sola,*
  I don't know if death is waiting for me too at the
gates of Córdoba, but it certainly does not await me in
your arms. When I die I shall be far away from you, but
at that moment I shall be closer to you than we have
ever been in our lives. Perhaps then we shall be on the
verge of meeting. You are my angel, the angel of my
life, my angel of death.
  I am not sad, Thea. I am happy. Only a villain or a
fool could love you and be unhappy at one and the
same time.

  Serranas de Cuenca
  Iban al pinar
  Unas por piñvones
  Otras por bailar.†

When you were walking in the elm grove yesterday,
alone, I thought you would start dancing between the
trees. But you leaned against a tree trunk and lit a cigarette. Don't smoke, Thea. And to set you a good example I shall give up smoking from this moment on.

---

  * Thea, far away and lonely
  † The girls of Cuenca/Went to the forest,/Some for pine cones,/
Others to dance.

13.

Santa, Santísima Thea,

I haven't written to you for ten months. What have you been thinking? What has been going through that lovely, clever head of yours? Now I am promoting you to the rank of saint and you are no doubt wondering at another of your crazy lover's mental fixations.

Ten months ago they fired two shots at me and both of them hit me. I am sure that at that moment a surprised smile appeared on my face, a stupid smile, no doubt. I distinctly remember thinking, Are we really about to meet? But other reactions immediately set in— shock and a terrible tumult in the body, which so often demands a vulgar and mocking precedence.

If I am still alive, it means that you are *santísima.* Accept this as a technical addition to the sum of your attributes.

We have good doctors and they stitched me up, but from a professional point of view my cover had been blown and my superiors asked me if I wanted to retire. Obviously I wanted to carry on because retirement would ground me thousands of miles away from you. And so that I would be able to carry on with my work I had to undergo a further operation that deprived me of my original face forever. Not really forever, of course. Because when our time comes we all revert to what we used to be. But meanwhile I am remolded and disguised for the rest of my time on earth.

This whole business does have one good side. I am now able to comply with your request of several years ago. The photograph in this envelope is of my face as it was until about a year ago. There you are, you asked for my photograph and now you have it. That was more or less the way I looked when you saw me, more than once, in the street and in other places.

Now I love you a little more. I didn't know it was possible.

On the last day of the month I shall be in your home town and you can send me a letter care of the post office. You will be in your provincial town at the university as agreed at 1700 hours.

14.

My darling, you are perhaps, after all, my only darling.

After seven years you show me your face, which is no longer your face. Have you ever thought, sanely, as other people think, about what you are inflicting on me?

But I should be ashamed of my wretched egotism when I consider what you have been through. After almost a year of silence from you I know what your letters, and indeed you yourself, are to me, if you really do exist. This year I have thought more than once that perhaps some office had been writing to me and perhaps this office had closed, as offices do. I thought in terms that I learned from you. But God is not an office, my darling. God has given you back. I nearly wrote "back to me." How ironic! Just think for a moment about what is happening in my room now. Your picture stands in front of me on the writing desk. I am twenty-five and I am looking at your face. How old are you? Thirty-five? Forty? You are good-looking, my darling. If you were to court me, the way that men court women, I would probably be bewildered at first; I would be afraid, but I would not be able to resist. I know that I'd be in your arms sooner or later. You are what they call a "lady killer." That's what you look like in the photograph, anyway. It's a pity that your hands are not visible in the photograph. I think I can guess their shape. But your eyes are enough for me. Do you know what kind of eyes you have? When I see leopards on television I am always afraid, but I am also full of admiration. I suppose the leopard is capable of giving his mate a warm, caressing, loving look even with a smile in his eyes. But as far as the rest of creation is concerned, the leopard has the eyes of a predator, a murderer, to use a frightening and confused expression. I think that you have honey-colored eyes. Am I right? From the photograph it is difficult to tell if your hair has gone gray or if it is light brown, but you are a really handsome man, and you know it, I think. I can just imagine how easily girls have fallen into your arms, so why are you so unhappy? I know you won't be angry with me if I tell you, for the hundredth time, that I can't accept your lunatic explanation that all your life you have been waiting for me and that all your life you have renounced all the opportunities that came your way. If you really have, then you are truly insane.

But you are not insane, my darling, I know that it's not true. In which case, what are you?

And now you have another face, but I am sure that they have not touched your eyes—you didn't let them damage your eyes—and I shall recognize you by those eyes. Please walk past me in the street again, as you say you have done many times before. You'll see that I shall stop you in the street, and so that you'll be convinced that I really have recognized you without a shadow of doubt, I shall fall into your arms without warning. I hope that you will be taken aback, but you must promise me that in such an event you will not act the stranger but will hug me and say, "You have won, Thea."

And then we shall see what happens. Don't be afraid, I shan't hand you over to the authorities. We'll go to some restaurant or other and have a chat. You have sent me such a lot of records and you have never sent me a recording of your voice, although I asked time and time again, years ago. Now that you have already bent the rules of conspiracy a little, please send me your voice.

For nearly eight years I have been reading your letters, but at times I wished you had never started writing to me. Now I want you never to stop. I have no doubt that we shall meet, despite all the circumstances, both known and unknown. And the time has also come for

you to explain why you chose Franz Kafka and why all
the music is by that one single composer.

Like a leopard's prey, I am yours,
Thea

15.

My love,

Your letter showed me a side of your personality that
I had not suspected, which is very embarrassing for me.
Now I realize that I am not the accomplished professional I thought I was. Haven't I always boasted to you
that I do not make mistakes about people, that I must
know people almost at a glance, because otherwise it
might cost me my life. And now it turns out that there
was something in you of which I knew nothing.

The way you interpreted the photograph that I sent
you, the conclusions you drew from looking at my eyes,
deserve a salute and a diploma! I am rather sorry that
you know something of my character, something that I
should have preferred to have kept hidden. But it's too
late now. What you saw, you read correctly. Luckily for
me you did not draw any far-reaching conclusions.
Luckily for me you liked my face. It seems that the office has equipped me with documents that slipped
through your examination because you are not suffi-
ciently well-trained.

At the same time I have no doubt that if we worked
together, you and I, we would make history in the an-
nals of international espionage. A nice joke! And an unnecessary one.

Thea, my Thea, lately it's been harder and harder for
me to bear what they have imposed upon us. I am almost tempted—in moments of weakness and heart-
break—to believe, with you, that we will indeed meet in
the end, in the way that you imagine. But if such a thing
were to happen, it would be a clear proof that I am not
worthy of you, that it was all a mistake. Because if you
and I are what I think we are, there is no need for us to

force the issue. The office will take care of it. And if it does not, that means there's no office. And if there's no office—how is it that you and I exist?

I am sending you a tape recording, as requested. I have recorded the second movement of a piano concerto, in which I am pleading, and the third movement of a quintet, in which I already know that there's no sense in pleading. This is my voice speaking to you.

And why Franz Kafka? I shall explain to you. I would have liked Kafka to be a friend of mine, and I believe, in my folly, that he might perhaps have agreed. He had a tremendous capacity for forgiving, he loved people and befriended even fools. I would stand a chance with him. You are, of course, entitled to ask why I did not choose our composer as a friend. The answer is that he had no need of friends. He was satisfied with his fellow billiard players, and I don't play billiards. Besides, he would have made a fool of me just as he made fools of them all. Did you know, Thea, that he is not really the composer of those melodies? They were all dictated to him from the office, and he just copied them down from memory. I was not keen to make friends with the office. I'm content with what it dictates to me about you. This dictation alone is a hint of what is liable to happen to a man who does not know his limits. And so I settled for Franz Kafka.

I have not touched my Spanish lessons for almost a whole year, so there will not be a single line of sense in this letter, apart from this last one:

I love you.

16.

My friend,

Forgive me if I have made a mistake. Forgive me for the terrible thing I am about to write. I only want to ask. You yourself drove me to this question.

I have read your letter and listened to the tape of 459

and 516 but I'm not going to write about that this time. I don't know how to begin.

In your letter there were no instructions for a reply. Nearly two months have gone by and you have left me alone with this, your last letter. I have not stopped thinking about the compliments you pay me on my detective abilities. You praise the way I explained the expression in your eyes, and at the same time you write that luckily for you I did not draw "far-reaching conclusions."

At first I took this as a straightforward compliment, but as the days went by I turned your words over in my mind. I went back to them again and again, as for years now, even in my sleep, I have been going back to the things you write to me.

This letter of mine will go into the box marked "Letters to Mr. Anonymous," like the first letters, more than eight years ago, but I hope that you will send me instructions for a reply, and then I hope I will have the courage to send it.

Tell me, and please be honest, because I have always believed your every word, tell me, did you have a hand in the death of G.R.?

Thea

17.

Unhappy man, my poor tortured man,

I'd be willing never to send the letter I put in the box, if only you would write. Nearly six months have gone by. Why do you remain silent? Please don't die, I beg you. Let me into your secret; I might want to go with you. I might want to leave you and tear up your letters. You can't treat me like this. I am not an office. I am a woman approaching her twenty-sixth year. Why do you demand so much of me?

I do not doubt your love, but I am not equal to love like this. It is as if I am your widow. You have no right to die and you have no right to remain silent. Tell me what I am to do.

18.

About a month later a visiting lecturer from Spain came to the university in the southern provincial town and he was introduced to the lecturer in Spanish literature. This was in the staff dining room, and when she saw the guest's face, Thea went pale and was unable to speak. The Spaniard looked at the lovely face with undisguised pleasure and asked if the lady was not feeling well. Thea mumbled something, excused herself, and went to her room.

The resemblance between the visitor from Spain and the photograph on her writing desk was remarkable, considering the fact that the man had undergone plastic surgery on his face. She studied the photograph and thought that the surgery seemed to have been concentrated specifically around the eyes, although she had believed and hoped that the surgeon would not touch them. The eyes were different, without a doubt. They were different in both outline and expression. As for their color—it was impossible to tell by looking at a black-and-white photograph. The Spanish visitor looked about forty. Apart from that, she knew nothing about him, for the time being.

Thea looked in the mirror and as she reached up to fix her hair she noticed that her hand was shaking. She took a Valium, lit a cigarette, and sat down on the sofa to wait until it was time for the evening meal. The visitor was to give a lecture after dinner. It can't be, Thea said to herself. It can't be. This man is a complete stranger to me.

Shortly before the meal, a man and a woman, two of Thea's friends, came into her room, full of good news. The handsome Spaniard had not stopped asking about her, and like a typical Spaniard, he was parading his feelings before anyone ready to listen, and here he was quoted: "You will be sorry you invited me here, because you won't be able to get rid of me until I can take your lecturer in Spanish literature away with me. She has broken my heart at first sight." An additional piece of news sent a shiver down Thea's spine: The man was not in fact Spanish, but a foreigner who had started lecturing in Madrid about six months earlier; his accent in Spanish bore this out.

As she went into the dining room she breathed freely again when she saw that his place at the table was some way from hers and that she would have time to study him from a distance, without being unduly embarrassed.

The resemblance to the photograph, which had struck her so forcibly at first, was not as great as she had previously thought. But it was impossible to completely ignore the outstanding shared features, which seemed unmistakable.

As he rose to speak, he looked at her ostentatiously, then he fixed his eyes on the notes in his hand and, in fact, read out what was written there. He spoke in the language of the country, with a foreign accent, but not a Spanish one. Thea knew that university teachers fell into one of two categories. There are those who begin with a witticism, and those who season the scientific text with quotations from the poets, even if the lecture is about economics or medicine. So she was not surprised when she realized that this man belonged to the second category, and since he came from Spain it was not surprising that he brought in Luis de Góngora between Hobbes and Keynes. All the same, her flesh crept when she heard that verse, especially as the lecturer glanced up from his notes when he quoted de Góngora, and looked at her. But he looked at her whenever he glanced up from his notes, and he did this all the time.

The lecture was entertaining, suitable for everyone, the sort of lecture that any intelligent and witty student might prepare in his second or third year. The man spoke fluently, was cheerful and jolly, and looked as if he was keeping further surprises up his sleeve for an appropriate moment. The paralysis that had taken hold of her loosened its grip a little, perhaps under the influence of the Valium, and she went up to him at the end of the lecture, smiled at him, and said, "I hear that you are telling everyone here about love at first sight. A big boy like you should be more polite."

The smile with which he had greeted her fell away from his lips.

"It seemed to me that my presence made you feel unwell. I am glad I was wrong," he said.

Since she had nothing to lose, Thea decided not to waste a

second. She looked straight into his eyes and said, "I shall ask you a question that young men usually ask the girls they meet in bars—haven't I seen you somewhere before?"

She thought he seemed saddened by her words and a light cloud darkened his face but quickly vanished. However, he answered calmly, emphasizing each word.

"My dear and lovely young lady, I feel as if I have known you all my life."

Thea examined his face closely and none too politely. She could find no trace of a scar, not on the lower jaw, on the neck, around the mouth, or near the ears. The skin around the eyes was fresh and slightly wrinkled at the corners as one would expect in a man of about forty. The resemblance to the photograph now seemed practically negligible to her.

A feeling of anger welled up inside her, anger that she had let herself be deceived by her imagination, that she was the victim of mischievous fantasies, the fruit of eight years of madness. Anyone might say to a girl, "I feel as if I have known you all my life." It's really nothing but a very banal expression. The man standing in front of her could be anyone, anyone but her anonymous friend. Nevertheless, she did not have the strength to abandon altogether the remotest possibility that might perhaps lie hidden in this meeting.

She said to him, "Listen. Circulate for a while, be nice to your hosts, and in about half an hour come to my room. But I'm warning you, I shall ask personal questions, unpleasant ones. If you don't want that, don't come. And no illusions please."

"I accept," he said, then bowed and left her.

She watched his back as he moved away. Sadness, resignation, and possibly even offense showed in his bearing. It was as if he were suddenly very tired.

19.

Thea placed a chair for her visitor opposite the photograph. When he arrived and sat down in the chair, Thea went into the kitchen to make coffee and peeped in through the curtain. The visitor did not look at the photograph at all, but gazed vacantly at the ceiling and waited patiently for her to come back.

"What do you think of that man?" She pointed at the picture.

He looked at the face in the photograph, then back at Thea, and asked if it was her father.

"Don't you think he looks like you?" she asked.

"If only I had a face like that," said the visitor. "He is an extremely good-looking man."

"Listen." Thea sat down opposite him and looked at him and the photograph alternately, able now for the first time to compare the two men, who were perhaps one. "Listen, are you a secret agent working for some country or other? Did they fire two shots at you a year and a half ago? Have they performed plastic surgery on your face? Answer yes or no."

The man did not smile at this onslaught and said nothing for a while.

Maybe he thinks I'm mad, thought Thea, and maybe he thinks that I am a secret agent. We'll soon know. It might even be him. God, is it really him?

"No," said the man at last. A smile appeared on his face and faded immediately.

"I don't owe you any explanation. I warned you," said Thea quickly. "Will you have a cup of coffee?"

"Yes, please. I see there's a piano here. Do you play?"

"And you—do you play?"

"Yes," he said.

"Tell me about yourself. Who are you?"

"You already know my name, but I'm willing to tell you more, and should even like to; and I understand that I have no right to ask questions, is that right?"

"You may ask as much as you like."

"We'll come to that, with your permission. Well, I was born to Greek parents in Alexandria. When I was a child my parents moved to Beirut. There I went to a secondary school and also the Academy of Music. My father wanted me to study law at the American University of Beirut and that is what I did. About twenty years ago my family moved to Europe and now I live and work in Madrid. If that is enough for you for the time being, permit me just one question."

Thea nodded assent.

"Those questions you asked me—were they taken from some information you received about me, or was it an attempt to establish my identity in order to trace someone you are looking for?"

"Explain yourself," said Thea.

"I can only guess. Could it be that you had some connection with a man who shrouded himself in secrecy and that you are trying to find out if I am that man?"

"Perhaps you will play me something you are fond of," said Thea.

The visitor sighed, smiled, rose from his chair, and sat down at the piano. He played about a quarter of the first movement of a Mozart sonata, stopped with a gesture of despair, and turned to her.

"I have lost some of the technique that I had when I was younger. At the academy I used to like playing concerti for piano and orchestra. That was some time ago."

"And do you know Franz Kafka?" Thea felt an immense weariness and told herself that this would be more than enough for the first evening.

"Everyone knows Kafka," said the visitor, "including myself, of course."

"Don't be angry with me, but you will have to go now," she said.

"Of course," he said. "I have been doing as I was told and I shall obey even now. I only ask for permission to say one thing before I go, and you must promise not to reply."

"Go ahead."

"You are the most beautiful woman I have ever seen. This in itself is nothing new to you. I know that you have heard it more than once. The only new thing I have to say is this—let me see you every day. Good night."

And the man went out of the room and closed the door behind him without a sound.

20.

Two months later the summer holidays began and Thea went to her home town with the visitor from Madrid. He was

given a room in her parents' flat and invited to spend a fortnight with them before he went back home.

On the third day of their visit, Thea, her parents, and the
visitor were sitting at tea in the drawing room. The summer
afternoon was set to continue late into the light northern
night, the windows overlooking the street were open, and
from below came the continuous hum of the rush-hour traffic
as people hurried homeward.

The hum of the traffic was pierced by the sound of a shot.
It was followed immediately by a second shot. Then they
heard the screeching of brakes, people's voices rose from the
street, and it was not long before they heard the siren of a
police car.

They put down their teacups, got up, and looked out of the
window.

Two policemen were holding the crowd back from the
door of the café on the other side of the road while two others went inside. An ambulance forced its way down the street
and stopped in front of the café door. The driver and his assistant took a stretcher from the ambulance and went inside
with it. They soon came out carrying a body covered with a
blanket.

Thea was seized with a violent fit of shivering and was put
to bed. When she did not calm down they called a doctor,
who administered a sedative, and she sank into a deep sleep.

The next day she refused to leave her room, insisting that
no one should go in and see her. She asked them to bring the
morning papers to her in bed. In the newspaper she saw a
photograph of a man with a mustache and a beard, his eyes
closed.

In the report it was said that no papers had been found on
the body of the murdered man and they were appealing to
the public for help in identifying him. It was also said that
the man had been killed by two shots fired by an assailant
who managed to escape. The murdered man had been sitting
by the window in the café. The proprietor said that the man
had been sitting there in the same place for the better part of
the day for three consecutive days. He had not seen the man
in his café before. It came out in the investigation that
several years earlier another man used to come to that café
occasionally, and he too used to sit at the same table by the

26

window for hours at a time. Indeed, it transpired that the regular customer of some years back used to pay a waiter, who had since died, a regular sum for some sort of information of an unknown nature. It seemed to the café proprietor—but he was not sure about it—that the payment had had something to do with women.

21.

Thea was ill for some time. She was feverish and delirious, but eventually recovered. The visitor from Madrid put off his return to his own country and stayed with the family an extra week. Her parents believed that his presence would speed up her recovery.

On her first day out of bed she went for a walk with the visitor. They walked in a nearby park and sat in silence on a bench in the warm sunlight. After a while Thea said that she was cold and they got up to go back home.

As they passed the local drugstore, Thea asked her companion to wait for her while she went in to buy some medicine.

When she told the chemist what she wanted, he rebuked her and condemned the reckless habits of the younger generation.

"If I hadn't known you since you were a little girl," said the chemist, "I wouldn't let you have this without a doctor's prescription." And holding the box in a bag he recited cheerfully, "My poverty but not my will consents."

Thea went back to the visitor, took his arm, smiled at him, and said, "And now I'm going home. I'm very tired and I want to sleep."

CHAPTER TWO

G.R.

1.

When G.R. was about twelve his father left home and went to live with another woman. His mother, who had suspected nothing until it was too late, was shocked. G.R. had sensed something not entirely clear to him at first, but when his father walked out he pieced together his memories and hated his father. This hatred soon gave way to longing and pain.

When his mother came out of hospital she was as beautiful as ever, but in her eyes there could be seen anger and dumb amazement, utterly devoid of curiosity. It was as though the woman G.R. had known all his life had died and he had now been given her double with no immediately discernible differences.

The strict, well-ordered domestic routines and habits of a prosperous business family, the meals at set times, the weekend guests, the journeys into the countryside during the holidays, the two trips abroad every year—to Switzerland and Spain—all these ended abruptly and were replaced by a hushed desolation. Beds left unmade all day long, a kitchen with scraps of food and dirty plates occupying every corner, a forgotten radio that droned on incessantly at one end of the corridor, a burned-out light bulb that left half the living room in permanent darkness when night fell, doors standing open in every room in the house, and the sound of frightened, strangled sobbing coming from where his mother stood, motionless, staring vacantly into space, her hands hanging limp at her side—all this surrounded G.R. for almost a year.

At first he would hurry to his mother when he heard her sobbing, stroke her hair, and in a whisper beg her not to cry, but she never returned his caress and her hands would remain limp at her sides, nervously playing with the hem of her dress, until the wailing subsided and she would twist herself away from his arms and turn silently and go into a corner, busying herself with some urgent matter that came into her mind: folding dirty napkins and putting them in a drawer or moving an empty flower vase from the table to a shelf of the sideboard. G.R. would follow her actions silently, not daring to cry, and finally he would go off to his bedroom and sit down to his homework. In the past she had urged him to work diligently at his lessons; and now he sought to do what once had been her will, although he knew that she no longer cared.

After a year his mother joined a religious sect and immersed herself in charitable works: She would visit the homes of the poor and go out at night distributing food to the tramps who slept under the bridges. At home a thin smile hovered over her face and her hands busied themselves once more with the little things that restored an air of normality to their flat, although for some unknown reason they gave G.R. a feeling not only of desolation but also of concealed fear: There was no point to the arrangements made in the enormous flat, for no one needed the drawing room anymore and the table with its twelve chairs and the two bedrooms intended for guests and relatives were always empty and the clean linen on the beds gave off a smell of death. In his mother's bedroom order was restored; half the double bed was neatly made up with the top of the blanket folded back in a little triangle and his father's slippers placed on the carpet, as if waiting for their master to come back from the shower. On the other half of the bed the crumpled pillow lay slightly askew in a sort of grimace of crushed anger and hope.

Once again his mother attended to all his needs and all that he heard from her revolved around the suffering of the down-and-outs, around God's hidden mercy, and the need to accept his judgment with love. G.R. would listen to her silently.

When he was about fourteen his father summoned him for a serious talk in a restaurant in the city and told him of his plans for G.R.'s future. Next autumn, said his father, G.R. would go to boarding school to complete his secondary education. On his eighteenth birthday his father would make him a present of a fine car and he would study at the university his father already had in mind; there he was to spend four years studying law and economics. After that he would go into his father's business as an apprentice, and from then on he could do as he pleased.

There and then his father gave him a present, in addition to the many he sent him every Christmas and birthday. This time it was a wristwatch made of a large and thick gold coin cut in two, the two halves forming a base and cover for one of the best Swiss watches, or at least the most expensive. When G.R. hesitated to touch the present, his father took hold of his arm, pushed back the sleeve of the boy's jacket, and fastened the watch on his wrist; and when he had finished, he gave his son a light tap on the palm of his hand by way of encouragement and said, "Well, that's that."

One evening as he was sitting in his room doing his homework he heard the sound of bare feet padding along the corridor. He looked up and saw his mother. She had just come out of the bathroom and had apparently not taken her dressing gown with her when she went in. Anyway, he saw her from behind, naked, padding hurriedly along toward her bedroom. Her body was freshly pink, the two halves of her buttocks danced to the movements of her heavy hips, from side to side and up and down, and she seemed to be supporting her breasts with both hands. Her legs were large but seemed light, as if they were thrown sideways. G.R. trembled all over and closed his eyes. When he opened them the corridor was empty and he heard the door of his parents' bedroom as it was slammed shut.

Soon after this his mother came out of the bedroom. She was dressed to go into town. She looked in at the door of his room, reminded him to be sure to eat some of the food she had left ready in the kitchen for his dinner, said good-bye, and went out. As soon as she had gone G.R. went to his bedroom window and drew back the curtains to peep into the street. He wanted to see if anyone was waiting for her down below and which way she would go. No one was waiting for her, and he saw her hurry across the street and head toward the main road. She walked rapidly, almost trotting. If she had not been dressed, he thought to himself, everyone would have seen what he had seen just now with his own eyes in the corridor of their home.

When he went to bed he could not sleep and late at night he heard the front door open and his mother's footsteps in the corridor. Then he heard the lavatory flush, a door close and another door open and shut again, and then silence. Only then did he realize that he had spent all those wakeful hours in bed in thoughts of jealousy, hurt, and fear. Now he relaxed and fell asleep. In his dream he got out of bed, went along the corridor, and entered his mother's bedroom, drew back the covers from her, and climbed into her bed. To his amazement she was not afraid but her face had a pleading expression, as if she were begging him not to do what she in fact wanted him to do, even though, God knows, it was forbidden. "Don't be afraid," he said to her, "I'll do it better than Father." Then she submitted to him and he took her, his embarrassment and guilt mixed with a savage violence. The look of pleading and begging for mercy that had not at first left her face gradually gave way to a willing and yielding smile. He woke from his dream wet and scared, but disappointed that it was only a dream. What would happen if I got up now and went to her, he asked himself.

In the morning at the breakfast table he looked at her sideways, distressed and hoping that everything that had happened would be forgotten.

2.

When the time came for G.R. to go to boarding school he was longing for the moment he would leave home. Toward the end of the summer, when the windows of the flat were opened at midday and left open until sunset, he caught sight of the girl who lived across the road on the same floor. He saw her standing at the window of her flat while her mother tied a black ribbon in her hair. She had hair the color of dark copper and to G.R. she looked stunningly beautiful. Very soon she found her way into his dreams, in which she and his mother were often interchangeable.

As he watched her from his window he would occasionally see her putting on her coat, and then he would dash down to the street and watch her as she came out of the house and disappeared in the direction of the main road. Eventually he came to know the times of her comings and goings. To avoid having to dash downstairs, he made a habit of going down early to sit in the café on the ground floor of his building. From there, through the large glass window, he would watch her going in and out.

By the time he went to boarding school he had a notebook written in his own hand full of his feelings of love for the girl with the black ribbon. This notebook even contained some poems that did not always rhyme very well. The day before he left he wrote: "I am not leaving you, my love. I shall come back one day and make you my wife."

With his arrival at boarding school a heavy curtain seemed to fall over his past. The new subjects, the fascination of the rigid traditions, the sports competitions and the exhausting training that preceded them, the different uniforms, the clannish pride in the sense of belonging to a school house—all these swept him off his feet and made him enthusiastic and grateful. He accepted bullying by the older boys as a matter of course and compensated for it by bullying those smaller than himself. It was not long before he found himself a friend after his own heart, a boy whose hair was the color of dark copper and whose eyes were a light brown like the heroine of his notebook. Their beds were next to each other in a room for four, and the two other boys had long been lovers in every way. On the first frosty night that winter his friend got into G.R.'s bed and said that on a night like this they would have to keep each other warm, otherwise they would freeze to death. They fell asleep happy in each other's arms.

The next day G.R. received a letter from his mother saying that in the spring she was going to get married to a respectable man of excellent character. She added that his father was annoyed about her decision, and although he had not refused to give her a divorce—something that had not been done so far because of her own refusal—he made it clear that he would not continue to support her financially. However, G.R. had no need to be alarmed by this, since he would of course continue to support his son. As for her, he was not to worry, since her fiancé was a man of some means.

G.R. read through the letter two or three times. With his eyes tightly shut in a grimace of pain and disgust, he conjured up a vividly detailed image of the man "of excellent character" and "of some means" doing to his mother—awake—what G.R. had done to her in his dreams and fantasies. G.R. struggled to summon up anything he could to dampen the rage and impotence that gripped him, but apart from his room- and bed-mate he came up with no remedy for his pain, and this remedy had nothing to it, absolutely nothing, until he suddenly remembered the girl with the black ribbon in her hair, the girl whom he had apparently almost completely forgotten since the day he came to boarding school. And she came willingly, with a soothing smile, and she tenderly wiped the cold sweat from his brow with her hand, put her cheek close to his, and in a whisper comforted him with things that could not immediately be translated into words. Yet they were appropriate, sane words, which initially breathed a little hope and calm and immediately afterward turned his despair into a profound joy, into a formal resolution that he made with himself there and then.

At night, as he lay in bed with his friend's arms around him, he tried to give him notice. This was, he said, the last time they would do this. G.R. swore that he would never love another boy and that he would always remember him with fondness all his life. That night the two boys wept in each other's arms and in the morning G.R. asked if he might move to another dormitory.

3.

In his last year at boarding school, when he was about eighteen, G.R. came home for a short holiday and was invited to a party at N.'s house. Entering the room, he saw his beloved sitting in an armchair and talking to another girl. He quickly looked away, went to the drinks table, and downed several glasses of alcohol. Then he looked around for a place from which he could watch her undisturbed, and he stayed there the whole evening. He inquired about her name; he had already drawn up several possibilities and hoped that one of them would be correct. When told that she was called Thea, he was glad that all his guesses had come to nothing, because the reality seemed much more beautiful. N. offered to introduce him to the girl, but he hastily replied that there was no need. "I shall get to know her on my own," he said, and immediately regretted his refusal, but at the same time he was full of a sense of pride quite new to him, because of his decisiveness.

The day before he returned to boarding school for the last term of the year, G.R. lay in wait for Thea in the doorway of her house. He knew that she was also about to go back for her final exams. When she came out of the house he smiled at her, and although his knees were shaking, he spoke in a voice that did not, he thought, betray his emotions.

"At the party at N.'s you saw that I was looking at you all the time. I saw that you saw and there's no point denying it, Miss Thea. My name is G.R. and you know that too, since you asked and they told you, 'That idiot staring at you all the time is called G.R.' Well, it's true. And now you will no doubt tell me that you are busy and that you don't have time to come to the café across the road with me and have something to drink, not even for a minute. Is that right?"

"You're very alert and talkative," said Thea. "At the party I thought that you were dumb. In honor of your recovery I'll have a cup of hot chocolate with you, but only for a quarter of an hour. I'm really in a hurry."

They went into the café opposite her parents' flat, on the ground floor of the building where G.R. lived. None of the tables was free, and as they looked around the room, someone noticed their predicament and with a wave of his hand suggested that they sit at his table, while he took his cup and asked another man if he might occupy the free chair at his table. G.R. thanked the man for his consideration and drew Thea, who had not noticed this act of courtesy, toward the empty table.

"And now I shall make the most of every second of the

quarter of an hour that you have devoted to me," said G.R. "Here is the first question: Did you notice that I watched you for a whole summer from the window opposite your flat? I live here, in this building, upstairs. . . . Didn't you see me watching you?"

Thea assured him that she had never noticed him. If she had, she said, she would have closed her window straight-away. Nosy and ill-mannered neighbors are such a nuisance.

"But I was watching you with admiration," claimed G.R. "Is admiration a nuisance?"

"You should have asked for permission," said Thea. Then she laughed and stuck the tip of her tongue in the cup of chocolate to test its temperature.

"In that case, I'm asking for permission now."

"Through the window—feel free," said Thea.

"And you won't close it?"

"I'm going away tomorrow, so it will be my mother's problem, and I think that she will be quite happy to acquire an admirer like you."

"You are cruel," said G.R., and his face took on an expression of sorrow and despair so quickly that Thea was alarmed and hastened to undo the damage.

"Please don't pull faces like that. Can't you see that I'm just defending myself against your onslaught? And now it's my turn to ask a question. Do you know why I agreed straightaway to come and sit here with you? I'll tell you why. It's because I think that you are the one who sent me a rather crazy letter. Admit it and explain yourself."

"Letter?" G.R. was dumbfounded. "I have never written to you. I mean, that's not quite true, I have written a whole notebook about you, but I didn't send it to you—it never occurred to me, before we met. What did it say in this letter of yours?"

Thea gave G.R.'s miserable face an amused yet serious look. She let a brief silence fall over them and then said, "I believe you. It wasn't you."

"And now you are sorry that you agreed to come and sit here with me?" he asked, his voice giving away his complete despair. He had now lost the courage that he had plucked up earlier when he stopped her in the street. He was sure that he was too late and that she had already given her heart to someone else, to the person who wrote letters to her.

"And now?" he appealed to her. "What's going to happen now?" He was unable to think of anything more cool and collected. Tomorrow they would both be going away and only after about three months would there be any prospect, if at all, of meeting again. He could not bear the thought that this first meeting had come to nothing; he knew that he had strayed completely from the secure and manly tracks that he had set out upon at the beginning of the meeting.

"My God," said Thea, and burst out laughing. "I'm surrounded by madmen."

"It's not madness on my part, Thea," said G.R. "For three years—more than three years—I have known you by sight—more than by sight, Thea. I don't have the right to use the words I should like to use. But I'm deadly serious."

"Don't be so serious," said Thea. "Tell me something nice before we say good-bye, since it's already time for me to go."

"I'll tell you what," said G.R., snatching at the invitation. "I'll tell you what—look, in three months' time I leave school and I shall have a fantastic car, a Jaguar, I think. . . . Will you promise me that I can take you for a ride in the car, to celebrate us both finishing school? . . . Promise?"

"Really?" Thea clicked her tongue. "A Jaguar, you say? Congratulations, Mr. Chauffeur. Do you mean that I shall sit in the back and you in the front while you drive me into the country?"

"There's no back seat in this Jaguar. Just two in front. It's a sports car," explained G.R.

"Ah, sport is another matter. With your permission we'll leave the offer open. Now you really mustn't be angry, but I'm already late."

They parted with a handshake, and when Thea was some distance away, G.R. kissed the palm of his hand and was happy.

From boarding school he sent Thea letters every day. He apologized for his stupidity, his bad manners, his unbecoming seriousness, and his feeblemindedness. ("Please forget the business about the Jaguar. I blush with shame when I think of the extent of my boorishness.") He asked only one thing of her—that she would not forbid him to write and that she would agree to meet him again when they finished school, in the same place, in the café that had witnessed the happiest moments of his life, the first happy moments in his whole life.

About once every ten days Thea would reply, urging him not to denigrate himself unduly, saying that she understood and that he was no worse than any other boy. Eventually she asked him to stop writing until the exams were over and promised that if he did, she would agree to meet him afterward in the same café and they would raise another cup of chocolate to celebrate their leaving school.

G.R. obeyed and stopped sending letters. The very fact that he had obtained from her a promise of a meeting seemed a sufficient achievement for the time being. From then on he turned to a further task that he envisaged as a kind of charm for the advancement of their relationship. He had promised himself that he would study diligently to achieve high marks in his final exams. It seemed to him that high marks would make a considerable impression on her.

At night, worn out by studying, he would draw the blankets over his head and summon up Thea for a talk. At first he would let her mock him a little, but soon he forced her to take his love seriously and she would allow him to stroke her cheek. Then he would pass the palm of his hand slowly from her temple toward her cheekbones and touch her mouth, groping like a blind man. He hoped that she would part her lips suddenly and bite his fingers, but she did not and so he would content himself with the sensation of gentle warmth that came from her lips and made his fingers tremble. When it came to masturbating he would dismiss the image of Thea and conjure up his mother's nakedness, sparing Thea's honor and keeping her nakedness in its purity for the day when its time came.

4.

G.R. achieved brilliant results in his exams, and his father, having looked at the certificate with evident pleasure, said without any hesitation how proud he was of his son. He promptly announced that, although he had originally intended to buy him a Jaguar, they should now both go to the show-room where his son could select the car of his choice. G.R. picked a cherry-red Lamborghini, a low-slung car with wide flat wheels and a flat tail that curved upward to stop the car lifting off the ground when speeding along at 165 miles an hour.

Over the telephone, as he was arranging a meeting with her, he abandoned all restraint and said to Thea, "After our first meeting I swore that I'd get good grades; that was all I could do at the time to prove to you. . . . It was all for you, Thea."

"Congratulations," she said, and he could hear her mouth twist into laughter. "I'm sure that you will bring the certificate with you when we meet."

From where he stood behind the door in the entrance to his building he saw Thea coming out to cross the street. He went out and waited for her in the café doorway, waving to her with his certificate rolled up in a cardboard tube. He knew that he was making a fool of himself, but all the same he felt that it would be impossible for her not to be impressed at the sight of his grades. When they had found a table and ordered two hot chocolates, Thea pointed to the tube and indicated that he should open it and show it to her.

Thea read the certificate slowly and G.R. watched her expression. Her beauty made him so dizzy that he no longer knew whether she was smiling with derision or admiration. Eventually she put down the certificate and looked at him.

"Incredible," said Thea, "and I was sure that you were more or less a dummy."

"I know you thought that I was an idiot," said G.R., happy and once more self-confident as at the beginning of their previous meeting. "And now that you see that even if I am an idiot, at least I am a talented idiot, and I may even have prospects of being a learned idiot."

"It's a good thing that I didn't bring my certificate," said Thea. "You would see how much better you are than me. You deserve a kiss."

As Thea leaned over toward him, he jerked up to meet her across the table, and it was pure chance that he did not crack her skull with his forehead as it was thrust out toward hers.

She kissed him on the mouth and they both fell back into their seats.

"Thea," G.R. almost shouted, "Thea, you did that, remember. You took the first step; now I'm not responsible." He tried to laugh, but his eyes filled with tears, and as he started to blink them back, his laugh came out all wrong and he took her hands and hid his face in them.

"Mr. Genius," whispered Thea, "all these people have not seen your certificate and they will just think that you are plain crazy." She did not draw back her hands but leaned over and pleaded, "This is impossible. Can't you see that it's impossible?"

G.R. sat up straight, let go of her hands, and picked up his cup of chocolate.

"Here's to the future, Thea. . . . You'll pay dearly for that kiss."

"You're a pig," said Thea, smiling as she raised her cup.

"And now," said G.R., "the time has come to introduce you to a certain lady. Come with me."

"What lady?" Thea's face became serious and her chin lifted a little. G.R. had not seen her look like that before, nor had he dreamed that her face could be so hard, but he refused to be alarmed.

"An Italian lady," he said calmly, "a noble Italian, and she has already been waiting for you for over a week."

"An Italian?"

"Princess Lamborghini," said G.R.

"Where is she waiting?"

"In the yard," said G.R., "just behind the building in the garage."

"You gave me a fright," said Thea as her face took on its familiar expression.

They went around the house into the yard and G.R. flung open the garage door. The hood, the nose of the red monster, was almost twice as big as the rest of the car. An enormous "T" was emblazoned on it, colored in gold and picked out with a fine black outline.

"Madam," G.R. addressed the car, "may I have the honor of presenting to you the young lady after whom you are named."

42

He opened the door of the car and said to Thea, "The princess invites us to enter."

"She's ugly as a toad," said Thea. "So this is what Daddy gives his genius son. . . . You have a very generous father."

"He's not as generous as he is rich," said G.R., but repented immediately and tried to make amends. "He promised . . . he had no choice . . . it's not quite as simple as that. . . . I should fill you in with the whole story, but let's forget, Thea. Let's go for a little ride in her."

On the main road G.R. drove silently, but when they had left the city and were on the highways heading north, he glanced at Thea and said, "Now!" He jammed his foot on the accelerator and got up to top speed in less than a minute; the car leaped forward into the passing lane and whistled relentlessly past scores of vehicles.

After they had been sweeping along like a tornado for about a quarter of an hour, Thea said something, but G.R. did not hear. As they passed one car after another a high-pitched whistle rose and fell in the small passengers' compartment of the car.

"What did you say?" shouted G.R.

She leaned a little toward him and shouted into his ear, "Where are we going?"

"Are you frightened?" yelled G.R., looking straight ahead.

"I'm not frightened," shouted Thea. "I love driving fast."

"Pity," yelled G.R. "I hoped that you might be frightened and cling to me in fear."

"You fastened me in with a seat belt, you nut!"

He leaned his cheek toward her while keeping both hands on the wheel.

Thea stroked his cheek with the back of her hand and said, "You've had more than enough in return for your grades, both from your father and from me. Where are we going?"

"To you!" cried G.R. "To your place in heaven, Thea. The heavens, even the heavens, are the Lord's; but the earth hath he given to the children of men, and we are traveling from earth to heaven. In a little while we shall take off, Thea, and we shall fly, fly, fly."

The stretch of road over which they were now driving was carved through a hill, the rock face towered up over them like a wall, and just beyond this stood a road sign advertising a restaurant one mile farther on.

"Before we fly," shouted Thea, "might I perhaps have something to eat?"

"We'll eat somewhere else," yelled G.R., "not in that dreadful hole."

"You've been making your plans without consulting me," shouted Thea. "Just remember that we have to go back to town soon."

"Phone them and tell them that you're celebrating leaving school. You can phone them in half an hour."

"You're out of your mind," shouted Thea. "This is unlawful abduction and I'll have nothing to do with criminals. I shan't speak to you until you stop."

G.R. turned into the parking lot advertised by the road sign and stopped. He freed himself from his seat belt and buried his face in the hollow of her neck and shoulder, kissed her neck, and whispered, "Thea, Thea."

She stroked his hair and said, "That's better, now you are being a good boy. If you let me out of your toad we'll be able to get something to eat."

"Phone them and say that you'll be back this evening . . . or if you like, this afternoon, but late this afternoon. Thea, I—"

"All right," she said. "This time I'll do as you wish, but I will know to beware of you. You're a violent criminal."

She went off to make her phone call and G.R. shut his eyes, leaned his head back on the headrest, and murmured, "God, God, it can't be, God, it can't be true, I don't believe it."

5.

Thea spent most of the summer on holiday with her parents. G.R. received several cards, but with no address on them for a reply, since the family was traveling by car from town to town, first in France and then in Italy. Toward the end of the summer holiday they met again and promised to write to each other, and Thea urged him "not to get carried away."

She said that the opening moves (such was her term for their relationship) had been too fast and now they had several years at university ahead of them and would each have an opportunity to "examine themselves."

"I passed the exams with flying colors," lamented G.R.

"But I am not a genius like you," replied Thea.

G.R. went off to university with a heavy heart, fearing the worst.

They met three times a year, during the holidays. In the first year Thea made their meetings conditional on their refraining from letter writing. In her opinion the written word distorted reality and letters had a tendency to stray into the realms of fantasy or even madness. G. R. had no choice; he accepted the condition. In the second year even Thea recognized the absurdity of the ban on writing, and in the third year they wrote to each other regularly. It was in the third year that G.R. plucked up the courage to tell Thea something of which she already knew the general outlines—his parents' divorce, the grudge he bore against his father, and his mother, who had, according to him, "caused unnecessary mental complications" by her "neuroses," as he termed them without going into details.

The same year, in the vacation before he graduated, they took his new Lamborghini (a white one—he had long since sold the "toad") over to France, and on the same day they drove to Le Crotoy, a fishing village in Normandy, left their belongings in a hotel, and went down to the beach. The low tide had taken the water almost a kilometer out and they followed the people collecting oysters, glancing silently at what they put into their baskets. They held hands and from time to time their fingers gripped tightly, as if seeking refuge from the impending night. Thea had guessed, from his vague and offhand hints, that a difficult time was in store for them, and G.R. knew that she had guessed.

To the amazement of both of them, their first night was such that Thea was inclined to explain away their difficulties by her partner's deep emotion, and G.R. was able to console himself that she was not completely disappointed and hoped for something better. Just as he was about to blurt out an appeal for forgiveness, Thea hushed him, calling him "my sweet idiot" and complimenting him on the beauty of his body and the strength of his muscles. She even went on to say that she had made him wait unreasonably long and she alone was to blame if his confidence had been impaired. He had only to remember that she was a young and foolish girl.

G.R. was so grateful that he could almost have cried, but he had the good sense not to burst into tears, and that very night he swore to himself that out of the first money he earned when he was working for his father, he would buy her a present that would take her breath away. He did not know what it would be, nor did he wish to consider the matter in detail yet. At the same time he thought perhaps there was no such thing as a present that would take her breath away. After all, it was her very levelheadedness that he himself had just received as a present.

They traveled around France for about three weeks and their last night in Aix-en-Provence was a night of stormy passion. Thea was proud of her triumph, and as she looked at her body in the bathroom mirror, she felt in accord with her femininity. She suddenly recalled a sentence or two from the letters she had been receiving over the last four years from an odd stranger who seemed wise but miserable. "It's not my fault," she said to her reflection in the mirror. "I have never even seen you, distant man."

When she returned to the bedroom she saw G.R. lying on his side, asleep, his face handsome and still. She kissed him on the forehead and he opened his eyes.

"My wife," whispered G.R., "my darling little wife."

"You'll have to introduce yourself to my parents," said Thea. "In our family you don't abduct girls, you ask for their hand."

6.

About a month before Thea and G.R.'s wedding was to take place, G.R. was sitting in the café below his flat and playing with the calculator in his hand. He was busy trying to figure out the accounts left over from an unfinished day's work, and Thea was not due for another half hour.

"Excuse me, sir." He heard a voice speaking near his table. "Might I sit and talk to you for a few minutes?"

G.R. was all set to apologize and to explain that he was waiting for someone, but the man's voice was extraordinarily pleasant, a deep and gentle voice with a foreign accent. G.R. looked up.

Before him stood a man of about forty, dressed in a brown woolen suit and wearing a soft felt hat, the only casual and relaxed sign in his overall neat and elegant appearance. He appeared well-groomed, forceful, and at the same time pleasant and friendly, and for a moment it seemed to G.R. that he might have seen him on the cinema screen or maybe just in the street and perhaps in that very café. Anyway he could not refuse. Moreover, in the split second when G.R. had glanced up at the stranger in front of him he had had another thought, fleeting but of stunning significance. He thought, if this man were my father I too could mature and age into such a splendid manly form!

"Please take a seat," said G.R., "but I have to meet someone here in about twenty minutes."

The stranger thanked him, introduced himself as Gyorg Milan, sat down at the table, took off his hat, and explained that he would not take more than a few minutes of his time and that the whole thing was nothing more than a little diversion. He was staying in this neighborhood on business, and he had already noticed on several occasions that G.R. had a white Lamborghini. He too was thinking of buying himself a new car and had already almost decided on a Lamborghini but had not had an opportunity to talk to an owner of such a car. Would it be too much of a nuisance if he were to ask some questions about its performance, if it was worth buying one, since it was very expensive, and what kind of service was it possible to get here should the need arise?

G.R. sang the praises of his car, recommended it wholeheartedly, and added that if the gentleman were free the next day at about the same time, they might meet by the garage in the yard of that very building and G.R. would be only too happy to let him give it a test run and see for himself, since these days it was not kept in stock and he would have to wait for weeks, if not months, before being able to try one out at the showroom.

Mr. Milan said that he did not know how to thank him for such a kindness and that he himself would never have gone as far as to make such a request; however, if it really was convenient, he would be in the yard of the building at exactly the same time the next day and he thanked him once more for this show of goodwill.

G.R. caught sight of Thea through the café window and waved to her. Mr. Milan promptly rose from his seat, put on his hat, apologized again for the intrusion, and turned to leave. He opened the door for Thea and said, "After you, miss."

"Thank you," she said and walked past him toward her fiancé's table.

The next day, as G.R. was going down the stairs of his building on his way to the garage in the yard, he told himself again that he had seen that man before, but he was completely unable to remember where or when. He had a fleeting memory of the man by a table in the café, but he immediately decided that his memory was playing a trick on him since he kept on recalling him in the same place he had met him the day before. Why on earth can't I get him out of my mind? wondered G.R. Is it because he is so pleasant? And suddenly a shiver ran down his spine, a slight shiver, a split second of a kind of dizziness. Yet I'm not afraid of him, he almost said out loud.

The stranger was already standing in the courtyard, looking toward G.R. and smiling.

They sat inside the car, with G.R. at the wheel and the stranger, wearing his hat, at his side. The car sailed out of the garage and into the street and then to the main road and out of town.

"When we reach the highway," said G.R., "I shall let you drive and then you'll see what she can do. Meanwhile I'll tell you a few things."

They both fastened their seat belts and headed north. G.R. demonstrated how the five gears worked, explained the dashboard and the coding of the colored lights on the dials. Proudly he pointed out that it could accelerate from zero to cruising speed in just twelve seconds. Mr. Milan listened attentively, and when they reached the access ramp to the highway, G.R. stopped and they changed seats. G.R. did not conceal his admiration of Mr. Milan's confident handling of the car right from the start. They flew along and G.R. could not take his eyes off the supremely calm way in which Milan gripped the steering wheel and the smooth precision with which he carried out the few maneuvers necessary when driving. When they arrived at a bar Milan turned into the parking lot and asked G.R. if he might buy him a drink. As they got out of the car he asked permission to have a look at the engine. The hood was raised and again there was no end to G.R.'s admiration for the way Milan checked the electric connections, the way he unscrewed the oil cap with expert fingers, the way he removed and replaced a screw here and there. No mechanic could have been more efficient. Yet this man about to buy himself a Lamborghini could not possibly be a garage mechanic.

They sat at the bar, and Mr. Milan sipped his drink in silence, his eyes fixed on the glass in his hand. G.R. wondered at the gloom that had suddenly descended over the man and privately attributed to him some of the thoughts that had passed through his own mind. This man was no longer young. Why, in fact, did he want a two-seater sports car? Probably he was not married and he enjoyed the company of young girls, but at his age such things could not offer great or lasting joy. Possibly he was suddenly having second thoughts and wondering whether the whole business was really worth his while.

Take me, for example, G.R. thought. In another year I shall sell my Lamborghini and buy a family car and we'll take the children in it. I could offer to sell him this car right now and he would save himself months of waiting, but it looks as if he already has had a change of heart.

"My young friend," said Mr. Milan suddenly, "don't be angry with me for putting you to so much trouble and robbing you of your precious time. I know I shouldn't have done what I have done. The selfish way in which I have behaved has been shameful and unforgivable. Tell me that you don't hold it against me."

G.R. hastened to assure him that he bore him no grudge, God forbid. On the contrary, he was pleased to have met him, nor was his time so precious these days since he was not working seriously now in any case. The truth was, he couldn't help saying, the truth was that he was getting married in a few weeks' time and was feeling on top of the world and so was happy if he could be of any assistance.

"Please excuse me," said Mr. Milan, glancing at his watch. "I must make a phone call now. I might have forgotten a meeting. Please don't take it amiss if I go to make a call. It won't take a moment."

G.R. looked at his watch too and was glad that they were going back to town.

Mr. Milan came back and said that it was as he had feared. He was to have met someone an hour previously and had completely forgotten about it.

G.R. offered to take him to the meeting immediately, but Mr. Milan said that on no account would he put him to any more trouble and that he had already ordered a taxi, and in any case the meeting was a long way away. G.R.'s entreaties were of no avail and they parted with a handshake and a few courtesies devoid of the gaiety that had prevailed at the beginning of their meeting.

G.R. got into his car and headed south. After about a quarter of an hour a taxi arrived at the bar and took Mr. Milan in the same direction. Halfway to town the taxi was forced to stop since the road was blocked by police cars, an ambulance, and vehicles that had stopped on account of an accident.

A white Lamborghini was lying crushed in a ditch, and when Mr. Milan went up to survey the accident from a distance, he saw a pool of blood at the side of the road and on a stretcher there was a body with a face as white as chalk.

The postmortem also concluded that the man had died from loss of blood.

CHAPTER THREE

Nikos
Trianda

1.

Nikos was the first offspring of the Triandaphilou family to be born in Alexandria. His father emigrated there as a boy from Greece at the beginning of the century, and his mother was also a native of Greece. A year after Nikos' birth his sister came into the world and in the course of time became a folk singer. Many years later when she started to sing in a nightclub in Beirut at about the age of eighteen, her father disinherited her, but when she achieved fame and her face looked out from the windows of record shops, her father sent her a diamond ring and without bothering to explain or apologize he attached a little note bearing three words: *Chapeau, ma petite.*

Money, fame, and reticence had gained for the father a position in the international community of the city and Nikos had engraved in his memory a sentence that he had heard from his father when he was a small boy, a sentence that the father had repeated regularly: "The true masters of Alexandria are not the bare-assed Egyptians but the Greeks, Italians, and Jews."

Nikos' first childhood friends were the children of the Jewish neighbors, from whom he learned to speak Ladino. This was not hard for him since he had learned French and Italian from his teachers. He was torn away from his friendship with the Jewish children at about the age of nine when his family moved—at the outbreak of the world war—from Egypt to Beirut, where one of his uncles had a bank and exchange business. It soon became clear to him that even in Beirut there were Ladino-speaking Jewish children in their neighborhood.

The daughter, whom the father intended to marry off to one of his cousins, and the son, whom he intended to take over his business, were both sent to the finest schools Beirut had to offer, and they also studied at the conservatoire, whose director was an old Jewish violinist. Triandaphilou the father was of the opinion that this could do no harm, but he was mistaken. When the daughter showed signs of excessive devotion to singing, the father took his two children away from the conservatoire and Nikos was told that he was to study law and economics and there was no point in his wasting his time on nonsense. At any rate, they did not prevent him from practicing the piano in the house.

The year in which his sister was banished completely from the bosom of the family Nikos went to study at the American University of Beirut. From the Triandaphilou family's point of view, the world war passed with them being close acquaintances of the Vichy officers, and they continued to amass wealth through all its upheavals, welcoming the Arabs, French, and Australians who were the conquerors of Lebanon before it attained its independence.

Inside their house antique icons still stood above his mother and father's bed, and on Sundays the whole family would kiss the hand of the priest with silver plaits and Mr. Triandaphilou would place a coin in the collection box and receive glowing words of thanks and flattery from the holy father.

In the privacy of his own room, while apparently working hard at his university studies, Nikos laid his own schemes. He learned ancient Greek, Latin, and Arabic, collected a small library of classical literature, and throughout all his years of study he would sit in bed and read Homer and Dante. He had ideas of his own, and his sister's fate taught him not to share his thoughts with anyone. Only with his mother did he have a secret understanding. As he sat at the piano when his father was not at home, his mother would watch him from her armchair and listen with damp and shining eyes. They did not need to talk to each other to know that the father was a nuisance and that the singing daughter was the only creature in the family who had openly raised the flag of rebellion, and she alone was worthy of praise. They both knew that playing the piano behind the tyrant's back was not particularly courageous, but this was at least a despairing whisper, perhaps a promise for the future.

When Nikos graduated he applied for, and received, a teaching post at his university. He told his father that one or two years of teaching would deepen his knowledge of the profession and better equip him for his role in business. His hidden intention was to save money and leave for Europe.

Luckily for him, his father was absorbed in preparing for a move to Geneva at the time, and it was not too good a moment to introduce his son to the yoke of business; therefore, he agreed with him for the time being. But the Swiss authorities refused to grant Triandaphilou a premanent residence permit and he settled for a move to Paris. This change took about a year, and when the family moved to Paris and settled down in their new flat, Nikos spent a few nights in it, then left a letter for his parents and disappeared.

2.

He set out for West Berlin, where his sister was. She could fulfill the promises she had made to him in her letters, and on the first evening after he arrived she introduced him to the manager of the cabaret where she sang. Nikos was to accompany her on the piano, and after he passed the test, he was taken on to work six evenings a week, from ten at night to two in the morning.

A room of his own was waiting for him in the pension where his sister lived, and knowing that he would not be able to sleep, he stretched out on the bed in his clothes and thought of how he had been reborn, how he was young and happy, and how he did not even resent his father. All the same he decided that in honor of the rebirth he would change his name and would henceforth be known as Nikos Trianda.

The following morning he left his room in the Charlottenburg to go into town, walking beneath the trees that lined the pavements. Spring was coming to a close; in the courtyards of the houses were cherry and apple trees that had begun to shed their blossoms and let them fall to the black earth, which was waiting to swallow them up, but which meanwhile granted the trembling flowers a little leisure to look like snowbells crowded around the foot of the trees. This northern ceremony captivated him for some time, but he soon found himself walking along the Kurfürstendamm and the large sign of the Kempinsky Hotel stretched just above him. He was to meet his sister there for lunch. All around him rose the sounds of the German language, familiar to him from films, and surprising in that they really resembled that jumble rising from a full belly and a fat throat exactly as the anti-Nazi films attempted to put it into the mouths of the baddies in the plot. Nikos knew that before long he too would be producing such sounds. Learning a new language is no big deal for us Levantines, he told himself with zest.

Anyway the sounds of German were the warning sign that was to be followed by many others, and at the end of this process Nikos left northern Europe for good and set out on the long journey south, or home, as he called it. But this happened some time later.

Meanwhile he walked along the pavements of springtime Berlin, intoxicated with the freedom that he was tasting for the first time in his life, and proud that all this freedom was something to boast about—the fruit of his rebellion, which had worked out so well. Almost too well and too quick.

His sister came onto the hotel balcony accompanied by a young man and a woman. The man, her lover, was the owner of an advertising agency and a partner in the cabaret where she was appearing. The young woman was the lover's sister.

Nikos was introduced to them and his sister announced that she would act as an interpreter. She spoke to Nikos in Greek so that they would be able to talk confidentially.

Nikos said to his sister that the German girl looked like a sow, she had eyes like a cow's although they were blue, and her hair was like faded grass dropped into a pot of pickled cucumbers.

"He said that your sister is very beautiful," his sister informed her lover, and to her brother she said in Greek,

"You'd be amazed to find out how good these sows are in bed."

"Do you deduce that from her brother?" said Nikos in Greek.

His sister pinched him hard on the cheek and said to the Germans that her brother was saying things that were untranslatable because he was a barbarian from the East and they would have to forgive him. And when they carried on talking in German, Nikos became fed up and said in English, "It occurred to me that we might have a common language after all, what do you think?"

Everyone was pleased with the discovery and from then on they started talking business. Nikos learned that his sister had contracts for appearances in several European capitals and that she was on the threshold of a new and extremely promising stage in her career. The owner of the advertising agency suggested that Nikos might be able to join his sister's tours as an accompanist. To this Nikos replied that he would prefer to stay in Berlin.

"He wants to go to the university," explained his sister.

"How nice," said the lover's sister.

"What for do you need it?" asked the lover.

Nikos contemplated the German girl's ample bosom, too big for her age; he contemplated her blue eyes, no doubt the ones sung about by the German poets when they described Gretchen, her white skin with pink blotches all over it looking as if she had just been beaten, and he hoped that the meal would come to an end as soon as possible.

And casting his eyes over the faces of those present, he smiled at his sister and thought, God, she's so like father! Why on earth don't they get on?

3.

From the end of March until the beginning of September Nikos devoted himself to the study of German and scarcely left his room. From morning on he would occupy himself with grammar and language exercises and set himself tests. He also gave himself marks and enjoyed seeing how much progress he was making. He was getting nine out of ten as early as July and in August he marked all his tests ten out of ten.

He did not see the city during the day, but at night he saw it twice—at nine-thirty on his way to the cabaret, as he chewed a bockwurst with mustard and forced his way along the crowded pavements, and at two in the morning as he strode along the almost empty streets to his room in the Charlottenburg—longing for his bed, where he would sink into nostalgia and go back to the shores of the Mediterranean.

Only in the autumn, when he had registered at the Free University and had found himself a supervisor for a doctorate in ancient history, did he once again start seeing the new world into which he had been thrown. Every day from the library on the fourth floor he gazed at the line of trees on the horizon and saw how autumn advanced over the treetops, turning the fabric of the branches into transparent lace, behind which stretched the gloomy landscapes of eastern Europe. He knew that somewhere beyond the horizon lay Poland and then Russia and all those endless regions bearing Slavic names. Nikos would open the window and breathe in the chill air carried from the east and believe that he sensed in his nostrils the smell of smoke from distant chimneys, and heard a murmur of life all at once foreign, seductive, and menacing. A small voice, which had grown steadily more powerful in the course of a few months, started whispering to him, and then shouting and crying out to him, to pluck himself up by the roots and get out of there.

German students, a few of whom he now knew more intimately, showed him that his sister had not been right; they were not good in bed as she had promised him. They lacked that trace of shyness and inner passion to be found in the girls in Beirut, nor did they have that memory of many generations of pious religious purity, sexual fears, and ancient atavisms that endowed their sacrifice with a flavor of an ardent secret and the sweetness of stolen fruits. The businesslike approach of the German girls put him off because in the face of their unconcealed readiness no opening was left for him to carry out his games of conquest and chivalry. At the end of the night he was in fact surprised that they did not state their price.

In the middle of a winter's day, at noon, as he went from the university to his room, a strong gale blew over the city. The blast of wind lasted two or three seconds and struck the people in the street without warning. Trees were pulled up by the roots, signs flew through the air, people were thrown to the pavement, and municipal trash cans and shredded newspaper stands were carried through the air like leaves. Nikos was thrust against the wall of a house, and he managed to grab hold of the door knocker before he could be thrown to the ground. The skin on his fingers was peeled and torn and his shoulder was hurt, but he stayed on his feet.

Then everything immediately reverted to what it had been before. In the evening the radio told of scores of dead and hundreds of injured all over northern Europe.

In his room Nikos dressed his wounds, made himself a hot drink, and lay down on his bed with a book in his hand. A smile spread over his face as he contemplated the possibility that he might have lost his life in this faraway place. Far away from where, he asked himself, far away from what?

An eye-scorching summer sun poured out its light onto the harbor wall of the city of his childhood and melted the air that hopped, skipped, and jumped to the sound of thousands of peddlers, thousands of café record players, thousands of voices rising by semitones and trilling guttural songs. The aroma of the cardamom in the tiny cups of coffee, the smoke of hookahs bubbling up through jars of water wafted up and was lost in the sharp smell of roast lamb turning on charcoal and dripping its fat with a sizzling sound. Lean and thirsty throats gulped down tamarind juice, their Adam's apples rising and falling, drinking from Hijazi brass tumblers stamped in silver with the verse, "There is no God but Allah"; the children of the Jewish neighbors called to him in Ladino and urged him to go down to the sea. He slipped out of the house and ran with them along the narrow avenue that offered no shade, and hand in hand like a line of satyrs set loose who had flung their sandals over their shoulders they burst into the warm blue water together, bared to the mad sun, squabbling in the heat of the fire pouring down from heaven, diving into the water with their clothes on, scooping up handfuls of shrimps from the clefts in the rocks and throwing wet seaweed at each other, bursting the pods that gave off a smell of salt, listening to the soggy explosions, and sinking happily on their backs into the shallow water.

At night, after dinner, lying in his bed (was that in Alexandria or in Beirut? it's all one) after his father had gone off to a nightclub with his friends and only the three of them were left—his mother, his sister, and himself—he would listen to his sister's singing: the words of a Greek song, a song of love and death, a continuous story with a repetitive tune consisting of an endlessly returning refrain, a well-mixed compound of a jumble of Jewish cantillation, Spanish flamenco, Neapolitan song, and some fragments from memory of the murmuring of a chorus from the ancient Greek tragedies. He was later to know—he already knew then—that these songs encompassed the whole Mediterranean, that they had started with the songs of the Phoenician sailors, those ancients who had pulled the oars and unfurled the sails and had set out thousands of years ago from the very shore whose waves now licked the fringes of their garden. Jews, Hellenes, Muslims, and Christians would come together and drift apart, slaughter one another and yearn for each other, and eventually leave the stage one after another. They would leave and return in cycles, in panic-stricken flight, with the sounds of calamity and destruction, the flash of warships going up in flames, the lamentation of mothers for their slain sons. And then there would be a prolonged silence, as if they were all rising from their graves and coming back in the smell of the roasting lamb, in the sound of the gramophones, in the tired, long, and despairing songs.

Tsor, Tsidon, Tel-Oz and Tel-On, Mar-Sela and Karta Hadashtha*—the bells of memories of philology chimed in the ears of the young Greek lying on his bed on the eastern border of northern Europe. As he remembered the sunshine of his childhood he shut his eyes and invoked the spirits to call up before him the wraith of the girl descended from these ancient peoples, the girl he intended for himself. What do you look like now, what is your voice and what color are your eyes as you sit at your window this very moment, somewhere

---

* That is, Tyre, Sidon, Toulouse, Toulon, Marseilles, Carthage.

in the world, despising the impotence spread among the new races and waiting for me, my sister, my bride? Your eyes are not blue, they are the eyes of a doe, but your body is white. Your hair is not the color of crushed flax but Damascus bronze. Please do not step outside the door of your house, for I am coming, I am on my way.

4.

At the end of his first year of study in Berlin he received a grant, left his work in the cabaret, and traveled to Italy. In Rome he continued working on his thesis for about another year and from there he traveled to Athens, where he completed his work. He submitted it in Berlin and was awarded a doctorate.

On meeting his sister he found her extremely excited. She had just received an expensive diamond ring from her father, accompanied by the note: *Chapeau, ma petite.* Her eyes were filled with tears and she showed the ring to her brother.

"I suggest that you send a few words in reply," said Nikos. "Write to him: *Je t'enmerde, papa.*"

However, the world-famous singer (Christina Vassiliadis was her stage name) told him that he was a fool, and on the same day she went to a jeweler to get a valuation for the ring.

Nikos went to Paris, saw his mother secretly, and promised to return soon. From there he went on a journey through North Africa, revisited his native city, and went to Israel via Cyprus, armed with the address of a Greek priest, a relative of his mother, who lived in the Old City of Jerusalem, and he stayed with him for several nights.

In the evenings, having returned from his trips around the city, he would sit down to eat with the priest, from whom he heard, night after night, of the cruelty of the Jews toward their Arab neighbors, of the need to put an end to the Zionist regime in Palestine, and of the duty of all Christians, especially Greeks, to join themselves to the holy cause. Nikos listened politely but was bored.

The day before he was to return to Europe two men appeared in his hotel room in Tel Aviv and asked him to accompany them. They assured him that it was only a formality and that he would be allowed to go free on the same day.

He was taken to an office, where behind a desk sat a man wearing dark glasses and whose face was adorned with a beard and a mustache. Nikos wanted to burst out laughing, but he appreciated that he would do better to behave politely, and the man, who offered him a seat opposite him, greeted him with words that surprised him.

"You are absolutely right, sir. The dark glasses hide my eyes, and my mustache and beard are both stuck on, as in the theater. But all the same I suggest that you take what I have to say seriously."

"Thank you for your frankness," said Nikos.

"It's not frankness," said the man, "just a simple security requirement, even if a little crude. May I see your papers?

"Why did you come to Israel?" the man resumed when he had returned Nikos' passport to him. He had a low, pleasant voice that sounded somewhat tired, although the man appeared well-built, muscular, strong, and very much at ease. From his English Nikos concluded that the man was educated, as far as he could tell, observant of grammatical rules and employing precise, carefully chosen words free from colloquialisms. Nikos was also aware that he would not please his interrogator if he said that he had come to see the Holy Land, like the majority of tourists, so he chose to give a proper explanation of his reasons for coming.

He spoke of his spheres of interest, his graduation, and his intention of becoming a teacher in some European university. Israel, he said, was an essential link in his journey around the Mediterranean, because he was preoccupied with the concept of the revival of the peoples of that region and he was pursuing signs that would prove to him that this rebirth was perhaps already standing at the gates of history.

"Such as?" said the interrogator.

"I could give you a number of examples," answered Nikos. "For instance, your restaurants. Olive oil with humus or broad beans, lamb roasted over charcoal, vine leaves stuffed with rice and meat, all these have been offered to me in Athens, Alexandria, Limassol, Jerusalem, and Tel Aviv. To the best of my knowledge they would also offer me this in

Damascus, Constantinople, and Tunis. Do I explain myself clearly enough?"

"Very well," said the interrogator. "And then, what?"

"And then I shall know that I am no longer a Levantine of Greek extraction, but the fruit of an ancient tree, which for the second time has sent forth a promising shoot of culture."

"Fine," said the interrogator. "And how does this tie in with the activities of the priest with whom you were staying in Jerusalem?"

"What activities?" asked Nikos, realizing that his mother's relative must be practicing what he preached. At last he grasped the reason for his being summoned there. He took a deep breath and laughed.

"The priest is a distant relative. I understand that you have suspicions about him. I'm sorry about that. I myself am unable to throw any light on the matter. I simply paid no attention to that side of things. It has nothing to do with me."

"He suggested that you should cooperate and that's what I want to hear about," said the interrogator.

"He suggested nothing, although he did talk about the suffering of the Arabs. That's true."

"And then?"

"Nothing," said Nikos.

"If you are suggesting that I should be satisfied with that," said the man, "you are just causing trouble for your friend. We are unable to take any action against you at the moment because you are a foreign national and the charges against you have not been substantiated. But we shall take harsh measures against him. If you had spoken honestly to me, we would have been prepared to settle for the priest's deportation to Greece, but if you are stubborn, he will pay for it. You can help him by telling us what we would like to hear from his mouth, and then there will be no need for us to detain him. He will just be deported to his country and that's all."

The snare set at his feet was primitive, but would have been effective enough if he had had anything to say. Now all he could do was try to convince his interrogator that he had no useful information to give him.

"I've seen this man for the first time in my life," he said, "and even that is only because I came to Jerusalem. It's quite

63

possible that I shall not see him again. I don't even know exactly how we are related. You are threatening me as if this man were my brother or father; and even if that were the case, I should not be able to satisfy you. I have no information whatsoever."

The interrogator sighed, then smiled and rose from his chair. Nikos also rose quickly and to his surprise he felt that he was not pleased that the interview had come to an end. He felt that he would have liked to stay on there a little longer. Nikos looked at the man's glasses and it seemed to him that the eyes behind the glasses were fixed steadily on him, and he felt that if he moved from his place the eyes of the stranger would not follow him but would continue to look at the place where he had been before, as if compelling him to return to his place. A not unpleasant shiver ran down his spine.

The stranger held out his hand to bid Nikos farewell, and as he clasped Nikos' hand, he said, "As far as we are concerned this meeting was completely superfluous, and I'm sorry if we have put you to any trouble. I hope that you will not be annoyed. It's not easy; things aren't going too well for us. Anyway, please accept my apologies. What you told me about the Mediterranean is a different matter, and it would be better if we could talk about that without a mustache and beard, but the devil knows when that will be. It was very nice to meet you and I'm sorry that it had to happen here and in this way. If we meet, I shall recognize you and maybe we shall yet have the opportunity to talk. . . . What are you doing on your last evening here?"

"I'm going to a concert."

"Which one?"

"Mozart quartets, in your museum."

"Ah, I see," said the stranger. "Well, enjoy yourself, and I apologize again."

Only then did the interrogator let go of Nikos' hand and accompany him to the door.

Nikos left with the feeling that he had let a kindred spirit go.

The victim clings to his murderer and falls in love with him, he said to himself, remembering some verse from the *Oresteia* and regretting that he did not have the chance to quote it to his interrogator.

5.

His wanderlust did not loosen its hold over him and for
about twelve years he moved from country to country and
from city to city, working as a tutor for a year or two in one
place and then moving on. His mother died without his meeting her again, and a few years later news of his father's death
also reached him. He would occasionally read about his sister
in newspapers; they had divided their parents' property between them through lawyers, by letters. He took a sabbatical,
rented a flat in Aix-en-Provence, and started writing a book.
He bought himself a piano but soon realized that the instrument no longer responded to him. All the same he played it
every day. When his sabbatical came to an end and he went
back to teaching, he made sure that he had a piano with him
in each of the flats he lived in.

He published a slim volume, in which he offered the world
his views on the revival of the Mediterranean peoples, but the
book made no impression in academic circles and the short
reviews printed about it said that it was "the fruit of romantic dreams rather than scientific thought worthy of serious attention."

When he was thirty-eight he obtained a lectureship in
Madrid and in the same year he was invited to give a series
of seminars at the university in a provincial town in the south
of England. In the staff room he saw a young woman aged
about twenty-five.

So here she is, he said, and his heart skipped a beat. He
was thrown into confusion, and casting aside the rules of etiquette turned to the first man he found and asked if the
woman was married or single. The Englishman, amused by
the behavior of this unrestrained southerner, answered his
question and offered to introduce him to her. Nikos shook
hands with her and sensed that a stupid smile was spreading
over his face while his lips trembled and his feet swayed under him. God, he said to himself, it's really her. Who had
been clever enough to call her Thea? Could she have been
called anything else?

To his astonishment—he almost shouted for joy when he saw this—Thea's face went pale and she excused herself from those present and left the room.

"You've confused her," said the Englishman to Nikos. "You don't often see a beauty like that."

"You will be sorry you invited me here," Nikos babbled, dazed, "because you won't be able to get rid of me until I can take your lecturer in Spanish literature away with me."

None of those present was surprised to hear this Latin speech. The man's behavior nicely fitted the image that English people held of Levantines.

After dinner, in the senior common room, when Nikos gave the opening lecture of his seminar, he did not take his eyes off her face, and at the end of the evening he once more decided that there had been no mistake.

When Thea invited him to her room after the lecture, he began to entertain the hope that she had also identified him with her own fantasy, but when she bombarded him with strange questions ("Are you a secret agent? Did they fire two shots at you? Have you had plastic surgery on your face? Do you know Franz Kafka?"), he did not think that she was mad but understood that she was trying to identify him with another man and that perhaps this other man was her dream just as she was his, so perhaps it was hopeless from the start. In the end she even forced him to sit at the piano and he was ashamed of the crudeness with which he played a short piece, not too difficult from a technical point of view, but which his fingers played embarrassingly badly.

As he left her room he pressed her to allow him to see her every day.

6.

Their subsequent meetings were no longer tense affairs and Thea said nothing more about secret agents and gunshots. Nikos amused her with stories about Alexandria and with Arabic songs. One day he turned up with spices, pulses, vegetables, and lamb from the market and prepared what he called a "Mediterranean meal" in her little kitchen. There was nothing new in the dishes, England being full to over-flowing with Eastern restaurants, but Nikos showed himself to be an excellent cook and she gave him that task to do at weekends to the delight of several of her friends in the faculty.

After these meals Nikos would sit at the piano and fill the room with the sounds of his sister's repertoire as he had learned it in Berlin, and in addition he would play pieces that he remembered from his childhood in Beirut and Alexandria. When the company was told that he was the brother of the celebrity Christina Vassiliadis, their happiness was complete. Someone brought one of her records from his room and Nikos listened to the tricks that she played with the songs from their childhood by giving them Western melodies and depriving them of their soul. He tried to explain this to the people in the room but quickly realized that if he sought understanding of the subject he was talking about he would have to start from the beginning. Over the course of several evenings he strove to show them the light increasingly breaking through from the Mediterranean, but he could see in their eyes what he had already seen in the reviews of his book; in their eyes he was a Latin romantic, a southerner, with impaired powers of analysis and an excess of saccharine Eastern sentimentality.

Thea sensed his distress, and when they were alone, she saw fit to comfort him by telling him that in her Christian blood—apart from other sorts of complex and devious inheritance—also flowed the blood of Jewish exiles from Spain who had come to England in the seventeenth century. At least, she said, that was the case on her father's side, which meant that she was more likely than the others to understand his spirit even if only dimly and by guesswork.

What she did not realize was that she had just given Nikos a final confirmation, the highest that he could ever wish for. For the first time since he saw her, he reached out to take her hands in his and to kiss them and press them to his chest while uttering words of thanks, as one thanks a doctor who has just saved one's life.

"Thank you for what?" said Thea. "Are you mad too? God, why do you send me nothing but madmen?"

That same day she told him something extremely general

and vague about the letters that she had been receiving for eight years now from an anonymous man, definitely a madman, even if a charming and clever one. "He's even handsome," she added with open pride. "Very," she added.

"And you thought that it was me," said Nikos, and his face was covered with sadness, like that of a child who expected a present but received a scolding.

"There's no need for you to be sorry about that." Thea laughed at the sight of the grimace of despair that distorted his face. "Did I not say that he was good-looking?"

Nikos turned to her writing desk and studied the photograph of the man, the photograph that he had seen the first time he came into the room. So, it was just as he had thought. Thea belonged to another. Now he looked at the photograph again and said, "We are not at all alike, Thea. How could you think that it was me?"

"It's a very complicated business," said Thea.

"But you are not complicated," Nikos almost shouted. "You are as simple as a goddess, Thea! What has happened to you, what has happened?"

She promised that one of these days she might tell him more.

When Nikos finished his seminar, he wrote to Madrid and informed them that he was putting off his return for a while. He took a flat not far from the university and told Thea that he would not move from there.

On Saturdays they would go out for a ride in her car, but on Sundays she sat in her room, busy with preparations for her classes. Sunday evenings were devoted to "Mediterranean meals" for the whole group of friends, grateful that Nikos had despaired of instructing them about the revival of his Mediterranean, while they all listened willingly to Greek, Arabic, Spanish, and Neapolitan songs.

When the summer vacation drew near, Nikos asked if Thea would agree to go on a journey south with him— "home," as he dubbed it—insisting that Thea, according to her origins, belonged to "his" family of peoples. "I want," he said, "to redeem the cyclamen from the northern greenhouse and to plant it among the rocks of its native land, on the slopes of the mountains of Lebanon."

"And what if the cyclamen doesn't want to? And what if

she does this to you?" said Thea, and stuck out her tongue at him.

"If you ever do that again"—Nikos imitated her defiant tone of voice—"I shall let myself go and I shall attack you and that will be the end of you."

Thea stuck out her tongue again, and the happy man realized that he had been foolish, hesitant, and unduly lost in a world of fantasy. He took her in his arms and covered her face with kisses.

7.

Instead of his journey south, they agreed to go to London, to her parents' house, since she had promised them that she would go to see them during the holiday. She also advised him to go to Madrid after about a fortnight to make peace with the administration of his university in order not to lose his position, and after that they would put their own affairs in order. They had the whole summer ahead of them.

In the few days they had left in the provincial town Thea told him a lot about the anonymous letter writer and also about her engagement to G.R.

In the end she decided simply to show him the letters themselves. It seemed to her that if after reading them he decided to leave her to her own devices, it followed that it was better sooner rather than later, and if he resolved to stay with her, he would at least know where they stood and would not be under any misapprehension. This decision was more an act of defense against things to come than a desire for truth and honesty—it was a sort of insurance policy for the future.

In the box Thea handed to Nikos there were over four hundred letters, typewritten, with no signature and no address. There was just a date at the top of every letter. Over a thousand pages lay in the box, silent and ominous. Nikos looked at them nervously and knew that he would not shut his eyes until he had finished reading each and every one. As he took the box and carried it to his room, he had the feeling that he was carrying a corpse, and perhaps explosives, hidden in the coffin, were about to put an end to what was more precious to him than anything. His thoughts were already revolving along lines drawn from stories about secret agents.

When he started to read the first letter and reached the sentence, "And therefore I love the country I serve, her mountains, her valleys, her dust and despair," he closed his eyes and said to himself that "mountains" and "dust" fit Palestine well, the country now called Israel, the country where he had been summoned to an interrogation over a dozen years before and where a sort of secret agent had interrogated him.

With the aid of his fantasy he soon started to understand how these letters surrounded Thea's life, so much so that they were a kind of overwhelming reality that had acquired a permanent place in the heart of their reader. His inflamed fantasy even alighted confidently on the very moment when Thea's heart was captured by love of the anonymous man. From then on he began composing in his imagination the replies Thea would have sent to her lover, and the letters that Nikos composed in her name hurt him much more than the fine words written by that tyrannical and invisible dreamer.

He read the whole night long and most of the next day, and in the evening he put the letters back in the box and went to the university. This time he was not cradling a corpse in his arms, or a coffin with a bomb hidden inside it. It was a verdict against which there was no appeal.

From the letters—and from the replies that were the fruit of Nikos' feverish fantasy—he knew that no man could take the place in her heart that had been acquired by the specter in the letters. If the anonymous man were to present himself as flesh and blood it would perhaps be possible to defeat him. Thea herself might despise him, but there was no wiping out an image formed of words and time, just as there was no destroying Nikos' own dream about the revival of the Mediterranean. No reality had the power to dispel a dream. No man alive can prevail against a ghost. Poor G.R. had tried and had paid for it with his life—there were no niceties involved in that. Nikos knew that he must be prepared for that, and he decided that he was ready. To die for Thea, he said to himself, would be much simpler than to live for her with the shadow of that man hovering over her day and night.

In the past half year the man had not written a single letter, thought Nikos. Maybe he had been shot at and killed? Or was he still brooding around somewhere, following us?

He did not hide his thought from Thea and for a long time they sat facing each other in the room upon which darkness had long since fallen.

"Are you hungry?" Thea finally asked in a whisper.

Nikos got up from his chair, drew Thea to the sofa, and they lay there in their clothes in silence, embracing each other in the darkness.

"Put your hands on my face," said Nikos. "Both your hands, Thea, my darling."

He soon fell asleep in her arms. She listened to the sound of his breathing and whispered to herself, "Jesus Christ, our good Lord, don't kill this man too. . . . You don't want my death, but I shall not live if you kill him as well. . . . Give me a sign. . . . Tell me, and I shall leave him alone, I shall order him to go home for ever. . . . Give me a sign, my God."

8.

God gave signs, long ago, only to his prophets, not to simple girls, even if they were as simple as goddesses, according to their lovers. The girls as simple as godesses listen to the signs that come from the recesses of their veins, from their youth, which leaves them with shouts of joy before they sink into old age and decay.

"*Olé, torero!*" Thea would whisper to her Greek matador now that they were lost, in the few nights left to them in the provincial town, in love play without end. Nikos was not like that unhappy boy, the late G.R., whose virility had been castrated at Eton and whose confidence had been restored to him at Oxford only so that he could amass wealth in his father's business and devote the rest of his castrated power to state affairs as a Conservative cabinet minister. Nikos Trianda was a wonderful man, a direct man, whose little touch of madness only added to his powers. What girl cares if her flesh is stirred in the name of the revival of the Mediterranean peoples? If that's what this revival is all about, long live the revival!

On one of these nights Thea asked: "Would you also kill a man out of your love for me?"

Nikos bit his lip and said that first of all he would kill her, and immediately added, "And then myself."

"And after that you would kill your rival. Is that right?" Thea concluded.

So she even despises me now in the name of the ghost and under his influence, Nikos said to himself, but he immediately returned to Thea.

After this they traveled to London and Nikos was given a room in her parents' house and invited to spend some time with them before he left for Madrid.

Separated from Thea, the scent of whose flesh had driven his nights wild, lying alone in her parents' guest room, Nikos went back to thinking about the letters, about the anonymous man, and about Thea's replies to his letters. In bed Nikos continued to compose letters of reply in her name by the score. He was a fluent writer but also consumed with desperation and fear.

In her room, at night, Thea also thought about the secret agent, and she returned to him with increased pangs, stronger than ever before. If you are alive, she would say to him, come to me, you must finally come to me at last. And if you are dead, give me a sign. You can't go on treating me like this.

But secret agents, like God, only give signs to their confidants. They are also very cruel and even unhappy, at times. At any rate, they keep quiet.

On the third day after their arrival in London, Thea, her parents, and the visitor were sitting at tea in the drawing room. The summer afternoon was set to continue late into the light northern night, the windows overlooking the street were open, and from below came the continuous hum of the rush-hour traffic as people hurried homeward.

The hum of the traffic was pierced by the sound of a shot. It was followed immediately by a second shot. They heard the screeching of brakes, people's voices rose from the street, and it was not long before they heard the siren of a police car.

They put down their teacups, got up, and looked out of the window.

Two policemen were holding the crowd back from the door of the café on the other side of the road while two others went inside. An ambulance forced its way down the street and stopped in front of the café door. The driver and his assistant took a stretcher from the ambulance and went inside with it. They soon came out carrying a body covered with a blanket.

Thea was seized with a violent fit of shivering and was put to bed. When she did not calm down they called a doctor, who administered a sedative, and she sank into a deep sleep.

The next day she refused to leave her room, insisting that no one should go in and see her. She asked them to bring the morning papers to her in bed.

Nikos also bought himself a newspaper and saw a photograph of a man with a mustache and beard. He recognized him at once. To make certain, he picked up a pen and drew two dark circles over the eyes like sunglasses, and then went back to contemplating the picture for a long time. Now there was no doubt about it.

Thea was ill for some time. She was feverish and delirious, but eventually she recovered. Nikos put off his return to Madrid and stayed with the family an extra week. Her parents believed that his presence would speed up her recovery.

On her first day out of bed she went out for a walk with Nikos. They walked in a nearby park and sat in silence on a bench in the warm sunlight. After a while Thea said that she was cold and they got up to go back home.

As they passed the local drugstore, she went in to buy some medicine, and when she came out, she took Nikos' arm and smiled at him and said, "And now I'm going home. I'm very tired and want to sleep."

On their return to the flat Nikos followed her up to her room, and locking the door behind them, he leaned against the wall and said in a whisper, "Thea, I don't want to live in a world without you. Give me the tablets." He nodded toward her coat pocket. "Give them to me, Thea."

Like a little girl caught lying and scolded, she gave a weak smile, pulled out the packet, and held it out to him, and he hastily hid it in his pocket.

"I can buy others," she whispered.

"Aren't two deaths enough, Thea? Do you really want four?"

She sank into his arms and sobbed on his chest. Nikos stroked her hair with his right hand and supported her with his left hand so that she would not collapse, clutching her tightly to his body. When her sobs subsided, he lay her down on her bed, covered her with a blanket, and sat on a chair near her head.

The next day he left for Madrid and agreed to promise her not to come until she called him, but he insisted on his right to telephone every day. Her father answered the first call that same night and said that she was well. She had already been in bed for several hours.

CHAPTER FOUR

Alexander Abramov

1.

One day in the winter of 1921 a real-estate agent from Tel Aviv arrived at a southern settlement in the coastal plain and acquired sixty acres of vine and almond plantations. He conducted negotiations with the various owners with suspicious haste, but since he wanted to buy land remote from the settlement, spreading over the summit of a low and isolated hill, he got what he wanted.

The settlement committee wanted to know the name of the buyer, but was obliged to make do with the assurance that he was a Jew. Even when the contracts were signed, his name was not known and all that the people saw were wagons beginning to roll up from the south, from the direction of the sandstone quarries, and unloading dressed building stone on the top of the hill. In no time at all a large shed was erected there and at the end of winter builders arrived and set to work. From the settlement they could see a spacious building springing up, climbing to a second floor, putting up a roof of red Marseilles tiles, and covering itself in pink plaster. Then a road was cleared, descending from the hill to the edge of the estate and, at the end, joining the road that cut through the settlement and passed between its houses. Finally the farmers were astonished to see the Arab workmen uproot about forty acres of vines and almonds from those that grew around the house, heap up their trunks, and set them on fire.

This work of building, road clearing, and uprooting went on for about six months, and one summer day wagons arrived, harnessed to horses, laden with large crates and furniture. The same day, in the afternoon, a black car arrived and climbed up the hill.

In the car, apart from the driver, sat a short, bald man of about sixty, with a dour expression on his face and a short, well-groomed, gray beard, and at his side a young woman, very tall and about twenty-something. The woman was pregnant.

It soon became known in the settlement that the couple had brought with them an Arab cook from Jerusalem, an Arab driver from Jaffa, and a young Jewish woman from Tel Aviv. The woman was a midwife hired to be a nursemaid for the child about to come into the world.

At the end of the summer a male child was born in the house on the hill.

Only when the manager of the winery was invited to the new house did it become known that the old man on the hill was a Russian speaker and that he spoke German to his young wife. In the opinion of the manager of the winery the woman was, to all appearances, a film star. Anyway, she was beautiful, much taller than her aged husband, and she moved about the house like a sort of queen, without a sound, serving the guests with excellent coffee and smiling. There was no knowing why they had built a house for themselves in a settlement in Palestine, especially since the man must be a millionaire as he was able to have a palace like that put up and fill it with the accoutrements of royalty. At any rate, the manager of the winery was invited to pass information on to them about the wine industry, about the conditions of membership in the cooperative, and about the prices of fertilizer, tools for work, and the hire of laborers. On the cleared area of forty acres the millionaire set out to plant an orange orchard. He assumed that many would follow his footsteps.

Even after four years the secret of the people who lived on the hill remained undeciphered. The house was now surrounded on all sides with citrus trees about to bear fruit. From the settlement they could now see only the red tiled roof dipping into dark foliage, like a kind of red flag rising up to the blue sky out of a dense mass of green festivity. The vines and almond trees planted on the slope facing the settlement were like the encampment of a defending army, determined to put a screen between the world and the house.

The old man and his young wife were seen occasionally as they went past in the car, taking the road toward Tel Aviv. Only the Arab cook would appear in the settlement nearly every day, buying milk, chickens, eggs, and vegetables from the farmers. In time even he stopped coming because the house on the hill now had a hen house, a vegetable garden, and some cows and goats. At the foot of the eastern slope of the hill, the slope that could not be seen from the settlement, a well was dug and an engine installed that announced its presence with a rhythmic sound throbbing in the distance. By now the millionaire no longer paid the settlement committee for water from the central well and this added grounds to the hidden resentment the farmers nursed against him, a vague resentment, the sort that people feel for someone who does not seek out their company.

From time to time the Arab driver would bring visitors to the house and take them back at night. In the upper windows, near the roof, the light of oil lamps could be seen burning late into the night. The strains of music carried through the stillness of the night and people who wondered about it said that this music was unheard of; the sounds of violin and piano came together in a melee, each outdoing the other.

2.

Abram Alexandrovitch Abramov was the son and grandson of timber and corn merchants who had warehouses and branches throughout the Dnieper region of the Ukraine. In his youth he had been educated by private tutors who lived in his parents' house; he studied French and excelled at mathematics. On his own initiative, and because his mother was an example, he wanted to learn to play the piano, and although this was usually reserved for girls, they did not refuse him, because he was his parents' only son and the apple of his mother's eye. In his teens he spent three years at the Kharkov

Polytechnic and was awarded a diploma in forestry, which was supposed to prepare him for the family business. He spent nearly twenty years in business, but about a year after the death of his father his mother also died and he saw himself free to spread his wings and go out into the other world, which was not Russian, which was not suffocating and melancholy, and where there were not so many muddy and dusty paths, where everything—carts, souls, and desires—sinks with amazing resignation, uttering a mournful note and disappearing. These things had not been to his liking for a long time.

He left a sum of money to the Russian woman who had borne him two daughters without the blessing of matrimony, and dried her tears with a batiste handkerchief fragrant with the scent of a French perfume, which he had taken out of his pocket and then replaced after carefully refolding it.

That was the second year of the twentieth century and Abram Alexandrovitch, then forty years old, headed for Switzerland, put his financial affairs in order, and went to Paris. He was as sturdy and as healthy as a young bull; he knew how to appreciate the delicacies of French cuisine and once he even went to a show where forty girls waved their legs in the air to the sound of shouts of joy from the orchestra and the clapping of hands. Nonetheless he did not see fit to peg himself down in Paris since his soul longed for the whole of the Western world. The forty years he had spent in Russia led him to believe that only now did he truly begin to live and no matter was so urgent that it could not wait until he had seen what the world had to offer him. His next stop was Germany and there, in Munich, he came across a nice bit of business. Sixty wagons loaded with railway sleepers had got stuck on their way to customers in Russia when the owner went bankrupt and the authorities seized them. Abramov redeemed the sleepers and sent them on to their destination and then he realized that in Germany it was possible to earn in one week what in Russia he had pocketed in about six months. So the Western world met up to all the hopes he had hung on it, and Germany seemed a place worth taking a look at, especially since Munich offered him an abundance of wonderful concerts, an excellent opera house, and the possibility of finding good musicians willing to include him as pianist in playing trios and quartets; and since

he invited the players to a splendid hotel suite, plied them
with fine meals, and dragged them along to shows, they were
not too particular about the quality of his playing and they
also agreed to play whatever he suggested. Music, apart from
business, and perhaps even more than it, was his chief
pleasure, Abramov told the violinist and the cellist, and they
had no reason to doubt his words. He missed not a few notes
and even got out of tempo, but he played with great warmth
of feeling, his face turning red and his brow dripping with
sweat. It was a pity that he had not worked harder at his
playing, the musicians told him. If he had devoted himself to
music he could have been a great pianist. Abramov agreed
with them wholeheartedly, but he himself was quite satisfied
with his basic technique. He had had no desire for a musical
career and asked only that music should not be pushed out of
his life. He loved it no less than he loved himself.

When it became clear to him that Berlin would have to be
his base if he wanted to continue doing business at the same
rate as he had begun, he went to great lengths to extract an
explicit promise from the violinist and the cellist that when
he sent them rail tickets they would come to him in Berlin to
continue what they had begun in Munich. He promised that
he would find a second violinist and a viola player if they
wanted to play quartets.

In Berlin he took a long-term lease on a flat and decorated
it with paintings by Menzel, Segantini, and Hodler. Thus he
brought Berlin itself into his house and also the forests and
trees that he loved. When his two friends came to him in Berlin, they found Abramov very pampered, settled in a pleasant
flat with a charming maid who fussed over them with effusive
courtesy, with a lace cap on her head and a dazzling white
apron clinging to her plump hips.

Without wasting any time they got down to work. To begin
with, Abramov played the "Kreutzer Sonata" with the violinist. They took a break and had something to eat and
promptly set about playing Schubert's two piano trios, one after the other. Only then was dinner served and after the
meal they went into town together, seeking masculine enter-
tainment.

Abramov knew that he was now leading a fit and proper
life. From time to time he guessed what was missing from his

life in order for it to be absolutely perfect, but he put it off for another day. He knew that he would live to a ripe old age. The baldness that had begun to creep up from his forehead merely added extra strength to his forceful expression, and the skull itself, which began to be revealed in its perfect roundness, gave his head the look of a battering ram, the sort that ancient armies used to cleave the walls of a besieged city.

He spent nearly twelve years in Berlin, and when he sensed what was about to happen, he transformed his wealth to Switzerland and sold his holdings of a currency that would shortly lose all its value. He himself reached Zurich in 1914 while there was still time. In exchange for a payment he obtained a residence permit and permission to buy himself a house on the road leading to Winterthur. He was fifty-two when he came to Zurich, hale and hearty, but he knew in his heart that the time had arrived to think about a purpose and to escape from the European plague. In Zurich he would wait for the storm to pass and then he would decide. He had already begun to think about Palestine. The West was in decline, and Herzl, the Hungarian doctor, had said some sensible things in his time, even if he did get lost in somewhat childish fantasies, for he was, after all, a story writer and an emotional journalist. Anyway, Palestine was worth looking over, and when the war came to an end, he would go there and see.

But when the war ended, Abram Abramov was preoccupied by a completely different matter. He was—as they say—in love. Not that he was in love boyishly; rather he had found a woman he desired and was prepared to marry him according to the law. She played violin in the Zurich Philharmonic Orchestra and he saw her dozens of times from his seat in the concert hall. He had time to study her thoroughly before he introduced himself.

She was about eighteen in 1918 and he was fifty-six, so there were certain difficulties, difficulties that could be surmounted if he behaved intelligently and carefully.

Ingeborg von Hase was a tall beauty, much more beautiful than was necessary to pluck a violin in an orchestra, and indeed upon investigation he found out that she had learned to play for pleasure at her parents' home and had never been meant to earn her living by playing, but the war had impoverished her family. What luck, Abramov said to himself. This is exactly what happened to me when I started out in Germany and found those sixty wagons of railway sleepers whose owners had gone bankrupt!

From then on he knew what to do. At first he thought that he should shave off his beard and mustache because they had grown too gray, but upon reflection in front of the mirror he realized that if he cut off all the hair growing on his head he would lose more than he gained. So he made do with pruning and cutting so that his face lost all vestige of the Jewish expression that the long beard had given it and took on a mixed appearance: Slav refined in the West. At least that was his opinion, and then he commenced action.

Using as middlemen some musicians who would come to his house to play ensemble, he induced her to come to his house for an evening of quartets followed by dinner at Baur au Lac. This seemed to him adequate as a first step. She saw the sort of house he had and it could not have escaped her notice that he paid more for the dinner than she earned in several months. The next step was a brief visit backstage during the interval to tell her that in his opinion she was completely wasted as a second violin in the orchestra. Why didn't she give up this career? She smiled and said that she did not have much choice and that she did in fact like playing. This, he said, she could do much better outside an orchestra, as he, for example, had done all his life. She smiled again and said that not everyone could have the fortune Mr. Abramov had. He raised his black eyebrows in surprise and commented that the young woman was of course greatly exaggerating and that she had her whole life ahead of her; if she wished, there was nothing that she could not get. He wished her good evening and returned to the auditorium. From his seat in the third row he did not take his eyes off her and saw that she noticed this. After that he left an interval of two weeks before appearing before her for the third time.

From then on Ingeborg von Hase and Abram Alexandrovitch Abramov dined together from time to time in town and on the other side of the lake in the little restaurants on the shore. She found him a charming conversationalist and thoroughly cosmopolitan, and when after several months she introduced him to her father (with only one leg, a monocle in his right eye, one daughter, and nothing else—that's all, Abramov decided upon seeing the man and on the strength of previous, reliable, and proven information), she said of Abramov that he was a patron of music and a pianist in his own right. Her father, evidently several years younger than Abramov, had also collected some bits of information about his daughter's elderly suitor and treated him graciously and fraternally. He also said that the world was not what it used to be and things formerly valued very highly were now completely different and we were all marching toward an entirely new era, perhaps freer and better. No one could know. We could only hope.

Abramov and Count von Hase met again, alone, the way men do when they have men's business to discuss. They lingered for many hours on the balcony of a lakeside hotel and ironed out everything necessary between them. Abramov, as was his custom, struck while the iron was hot and concluded a deal. The most successful deal of his life.

At the end of 1920 he married Ingeborg and together they went on a short visit to Palestine.

In 1921 they went back again to have a house built. She agreed with him that people like themselves do well to go out into the desert, to an unknown land, among the naïve and foreign people who, just like them, were opening a new page in their lives. Both of them promised each other that music would fill the gap left in their hearts by the memories of their beloved but declining Europe.

Ingeborg's father was given the fine house on the road leading to Winterthur. "You will always be welcome guests if you want to come back here," he told the couple as they bade him farewell.

3.

When their son, Alexander, was born and the midwife held up the swaddled figure in front of his father, Abram Alexandrovitch placed his short thick finger in the palm of the baby's hand and the latter gripped it tightly.

"He has the fingers of a cellist, Inge," he told his wife. "Soon we shall be able to play trios in the family."

The woman who had given birth smiled at her husband but immediately burst into tears.

"You mustn't give him glass to eat," she wailed, "he'll hurt himself and bleed."

Further signs of mental disorder appeared in Ingeborg in the days to come. She would be silent for hours on end, cry with her eyes shut, and utter confused words, even when she was cheerful. The doctor calmed Abram Alexandrovitch and assured him that this was a passing phenomenon, but even when the symptoms had gone and Ingeborg was her old self again—a woman who moved silently about the house, smiling and doing the housework, supervising the cook and the maid and breast-feeding her son—the fear in her husband's heart did not fade away. He saw in this a hint that the fortune that had smiled on him all his life was now betraying him. From beneath his bushy black eyebrows he followed his wife's movements, trying to detect the signs that had apparently escaped him until now. Fearing his constant gaze, Ingeborg walked even slower and quieter, as if to say: I don't mean to hide anything from you. On the contrary, I'm walking slower so that you will be able to see everything you want.

In time the husband agreed to forget what had happened after the birth and their lives returned to normal.

By the time Alexander was five he spoke a mixture of four languages: Russian, in which his father took great care to read him some of the folk tales from his library; German, which he spoke with his mother; Hebrew, which he picked up from his nurse; and Arabic, which he heard from the maid, the cook, and the driver.

His parents bought him a small cello and a music teacher used to come from Tel Aviv twice a week. Alexander loved the cello and played with it as if it were a toy, a toy that responded generously to the musical talent he had inherited from his parents. But there were other toys besides the cello to which he was no less devoted. His father's shotgun and the noise it made when his father shot at rabbits, foxes, and partridges was just as enchanting to him as the sounds he made with his cello. Those sounds would make the little animals spring up into the air before they plunged down, giving one last little twitch and immediately becoming as silent as a clod of earth. At the sight of these exploits, little Alexander would gaze admiringly at his father, who took this as a sign that they were going to be good friends in due course.

He had a horse of his own, and accompanied by his mother, he used to go out riding along the path from which the vines had been cleared to allow them to ride side by side around the estate. The Arab driver taught him to swim and dive into the pool where the water for irrigating the orchard was stored, and the cook used to give him a reward of one farthing for every pigeon he caught, on condition that he caught it with his own hands and brought it to him still alive.

In the almond-shelling season, when scores of Arab women would sit in the farmyard and peel the dry skins off the yellow almonds with their fingers and throw them into bins while their children ran about, Alexander would pick two or three children he liked and go off with them into the orchard, where they would scratch around in the mole hills to find where the moles hid; when they spotted a hare they chased it until it disappeared from sight and once they managed to crush the head of a black snake and brought its long corpse hanging from a pole and frightened the women workers, who fled screaming for their lives.

His father told him about the settlement that spread out below to the west, and about its inhabitants, and he knew that they were "simple," ignorant people who ate with their hands and "did not wash." They were unfortunate people, said the father, and they were not to be blamed, but neither should one mix with them.

His mother said that they might be good people but they were "consumed with jealousy" and very dangerous. The cook said that they all cheated and gave short weight; they were also "misers" and "dung eaters."

Only the nurse revealed to him secretly that when he grew up and went to school he would know nice, good boys like himself and would have many friends. This promise filled him with both curiosity and grave apprehensions.

Meanwhile, he stayed in the house on the hill, sat down at the dinner table in a blue and white sailor suit, with its wide square collar folded down over his back, and dined in the company of two or three strangers who came from the city several times a week and played music with Mother and Father.

Alexander would withdraw to his room. They would leave the door open and it was agreed that he might listen to the music as much as he wanted until he fell asleep. He would listen to the tunes coming from the drawing room with his eyes fixed upon the opposite wall. On the wall hung an engraving that had been sent to them as a present from Paris and it showed a monster with the head of a bull and the body of a man, down on its knees in an arena, about to die. From a ringside seat a woman reached out her hand as if trying to touch the dying head; a small distance remained between the extended hand and the huge head, and Alexander knew that if the hand were to touch the head the dying creature would be saved. He waited for a long time, perhaps a miracle would occur and the hand would touch the head after all, but the miracle did not occur and Alexander shut his eyes. As he closed his eyes he would see, as if from the side, how he pierced the first circle of the music, and he entered and lingered there for a while. Then he would pierce the second circle and he would already be close to the center; finally he would pierce the third circle—and immediately fall asleep. To be awake in the center of the music was impossible, since it was dangerous and beyond the powers of anyone, whoever he might be; even grown-ups could not withstand it. This was already clear to him then, and in the course of time it became even clearer.

4.

When Alexander was six years old it seemed that there was no choice but to send him to school in the settlement. The method by which his mother and father had received their education was no longer possible. Even if they had wanted they could not have obtained good tutors who would agree to come and live with them. This country, whose climate was so pleasant and whose fruit was excellent, was still inhabited by primitive people and the price had to be paid.

He was taken to the school dressed in his well-ironed sailor suit, and his nurse introduced him to the teacher and did not leave until she had seen that they seated him in a good place in the middle of the second row, next to a girl dressed in clean clothes.

Alexander did not look at his neighbor even once. From the moment he sat in his place until the bell rang he did not take his eyes off the teacher. Not once did he blink and eventually the teacher avoided looking in his direction, because he felt slightly dizzy under the gaze that seemed to him troublesome and annoying.

During the break Alexander left the class with a hurried step, went over to the trunk of a eucalyptus tree in the yard, and leaned his back against it and observed the confusion in front of him. A group of children from a higher class clustered around him. There were boys of eight and nine and they whispered among themselves and chuckled. Suddenly one of them said to him, "Your mother's a goy and you're a goy yourself, you shitty millionaire."

Alexander leaped at the boy and thumped him on the chest. The members of the gang immediately fell upon him and started hitting him, kicking and tearing the sailor's collar from his back, pulling his hair and scratching him. Alexander defended himself as best he could and managed to knock one of them to the ground. This boy hurt himself on a stone and burst into tears. For a moment the children retreated a step or two and Alexander stood facing them, his legs apart and his fists clenched.

The children looked at him. His suit was torn, blood was pouring from his cheek, and his legs had been bruised by kicks. The children expected him finally to burst into tears, but he stood motionless facing them, and he looked at them as he had looked at his teacher during the lesson: without tears, without even hatred or anger. Only curiosity showed in his eyes, and something else that frightened the children.

His big eyes, slightly more elongated than was usual, remained wide open, unblinking. Their color, a mixed inheritance of the brown of his father's and the green of his mother's, was light and dark at the same time, and streaks of greenish gold furrowed them from the pupil to the iris, which did not move or even quiver.

A man runs into eyes like these when he is chasing a hare

in the darkness of the orchard, but when he catches up with it and it turns its skull to him, it is not a hare in front of him but a lion cub. And the man runs in fear of his life. That was how the children fled when they had stood on the spot for a few seconds. They did not know what it was that they were afraid of, nor did they understand why they took to their heels and fled.

Alexander turned toward the school gate and went home.

His father summoned the headmaster and demanded that the "juvenile delinquents" be properly punished. When the headmaster had gone, Alexander was asked if he would agree to go back to school the next day. When his mother tried to dissuade him, Abramov gestured to her to keep quiet and she pursed her lips and the mute smile reappeared on her face.

"Of course," said Alexander. "If they come again I shall kill them."

"That's my boy," said his father, "don't give in."

And the next day Alexander went back to the class. He sat in his place, next to the girl of the day before, did not look at her, and once more fixed his eyes on the teacher and did not take them off him until the bell rang.

During the break he leaned his back against the eucalyptus trunk in the yard and no child came near him. Not on that day or on the many days that followed.

It was only after a few months, after the Passover holiday, when the bell rang for the main break, that he turned for the first time to his neighbor and said to her, "Take this. My mother's giving it to you as a present." He handed the girl a parcel containing a big apple cake. His mother had sent the present after Alexander had told her that his neighbor was a good girl, diligently attended to her studies, and did not have lice in her hair.

5.

After the second year at school, at the end of the summer, the Arabs attacked the Jewish towns and settlements. In Hebron about fifty students at a Jewish theological seminary were slaughtered, in Jaffa several Jews who had not managed to escape to Tel Aviv were murdered, and onslaughts were made on the settlements from the wadis and nearby orchards.

For the first time strangers from the settlement were allowed access to the house on the hill. The Haganah command informed Abram Abramov that they had to set up a defense position on the hill and that six young men would stay there on a permanent basis until the attacks ceased. He consented and even announced that he had his own shotgun and was prepared to join them in guard duty.

The Arab maid went to her village in accordance with her husband's demand, but the driver and the cook stayed on. The cook, at Ingeborg's instructions, made hot meals for the men and took them to the post.

Sandbags were piled up at the top of the eastern slope and arranged in a semicircle. Behind the sandbags they placed three mattresses upon which three of the six men were always sleeping while the other three were stationed there with their weapons.

The warm summer nights absolved the Abramovs from inviting the men to sleep inside the house, but Ingeborg told her husband that if the events continued into the winter they would have to give the defenders a room in the house.

Four men from the settlement were killed in an ambush and about two weeks later another one was killed and several were wounded. From the hill the Abramovs saw the funeral processions moving toward the cemetery and Abramov said, "That's the price we have to pay. You can't do anything about it, this is a primitive country."

In the evenings they continued to play music in the house, even if the musicians from Tel Aviv could not come. At the beginning of winter, life returned to normal in the settlement and throughout the country.

When he went back to school for the third year, Alexander learned that the father of his neighbor was one of those killed. During the break he went up to her and said that when he grew up he would avenge her father's blood. He went on to say that she had to believe him, and wanted to know if she did believe him. She assured him that she believed him.

Alexander told his parents about what had happened to his friend and asked what they intended to do about it. Ingeborg and Abram looked at each other and said nothing for a while, but Alexander demanded an answer.

"What do you suggest?" asked his father.

"That you should go to her mother and give her money to buy food," said Alexander.

"What makes you think that they don't have any money?"

"Because her father is dead and there's no one to work and earn any."

"Very well, we'll see," said his father, and that very day he went with his driver to the widow's house. The astonished woman burst into tears, thanked him effusively, and said that she had had no idea that he was such a good man, but she did not need any assistance, for the settlement committee was taking care of compensation for her and in the meantime her brother-in-law was seeing to all their needs.

Abramov returned home and reported to his wife and son. Privately he wondered where his son had got ideas like that and where he had learned compassion. It occurred to him that never in his life had he roused himself to help a fellow human being. It was true that he had put a decent sum of money into the hands of a Russian woman many years before, but at the time he had seen it as a sort of payment for certain pleasures and services rendered. He had never been in debt to anyone, of course, but neither had he given when there had not been a good reason to do so. Abramov looked at his son very closely, stroked his head, hugged him, and patted him on the shoulder.

"Well, fine," he said. "We've done what you asked."

6.

They celebrated his thirteenth birthday with a special meal, after which they played a Shubert trio that they had rehearsed frequently. Alexander had been given permission to invite anyone he wanted to the meal, as long as he remembered that he was not to fill the house with cheeky urchins.

Alexander wanted to invite his classmate and her alone. When asked if he would invite her mother as well, he said that there was no need.

She arrived punctually and brought him a book of poems by Bialik as a present. He introduced her to his parents. Her name was Leah and she was a plump and pleasant-looking girl who blushed at every question addressed to her and became intimidated by what she saw. Throughout the meal she sat without uttering a sound, and when she was left alone on the sofa—an audience of one—watching the three players with curiosity, she held her breath and bit her lips. She listened to them until they had finished playing, got down from the sofa, and whispered into Ingeborg's ear that she wanted to wee-wee. When she came back into the room, Abramov asked her what she had thought of the music.

"The nicest song was the one Alex played," she said. "He played it right in the middle."

"Alex?" Abramov laughed. "Is his name Alex?"

"That's what they call me and I don't mind it," explained Alexander.

He accompanied her home in their car. On the way he explained that he was not yet up to playing music like that, but his father had insisted on it. But when he grew up he would play marvelously. He said that when he grew up he would be an international cellist. Leah said that he already played marvelously.

He got out of the car to go with her to the end of the path leading to her house and there he said to her, "Now I want to give you a kiss, in honor of my birthday."

They firmly puckered their lips, kissed each other, and separated immediately.

When he went back to the car the driver told him that he had seen what they had done and in his opinion they had not behaved properly. His mother and father would be angry if they knew. To this Alexander replied that there was a big difference between Jews and Arabs and, besides, he intended to marry this girl when he grew up and had avenged her father's blood.

"How will you know who murdered him?" objected the driver.

"I shall know all right," Alexander assured him. "You can rely on me."

7.

In his last year at primary school Alexander stood about a head taller than all the other children in the class. Now he sat alone on a double bench whose other seat was empty. After the kiss with Leah he had moved from the shared bench but he still hung around with her in the breaks, in a corner of their own. No boys spoke to Leah and only the girls had the right to address her. They all knew that Alex had "bought" her, since he was a millionaire, but Leah did not care. She was just waiting for the day when she could obey all his wishes, and then she would be happy and would want nothing more.

That year Alexander read dozens of books from his father's library, which now included books in Russian, German, and Hebrew. He had a secret diary in which he would write down various things and that year he made a note for himself of four books that had made a profound impression on him.

> *Kreutzer Sonta* by Tolstoy is a very interesting book, because he explains to the reader that married life is very dangerous for people, and even music is dangerous, but I am sure that it is possible to overcome that. I do not yet know how, but I think that it is possible. Anyway the author understands music.
>
> *Mozart and Salieri* by Pushkin proves that if a man is a criminal he cannot be a good musician or a true artist at all. I think that Pushkin was right.
>
> *Michael Kohlhaas* by Kleist shows that if you want to be just and to take revenge on your enemies, you have to remember that there is a limit. It is impossible simply to kill hundreds of men on account of some horses. I have thought about this a lot, because at first I decided that when I go to avenge the blood of Leah's father I should kill ten Arabs and settle the account. But now I see that I shall have to discover the real murderer and kill only him; otherwise, what happened to Kolhaus will happen to me. I mean the mistake he made.

The most interesting book I have read so far is *Don Quixote* by Cervantes. It is the most interesting because, first of all, it is funny and also I cried when I read how Don Quixote makes a speech to the shepherds and also when he dies at the end, and in some other places. I also laughed a lot in all sorts of places. I think that this book tells about everyone, even my father or myself. Sometimes you are Don Quixote and sometimes you are Sancho Panza and sometimes you are both of them at the same time. That is a very profound idea and I think that the author is definitely right. The author is the most talented that I have read so far, and even Father agrees with me. Mother likes Goethe most of all and I have read *The Sufferings of Young Werther*. It is not a bad book but I could not continue with *Faust* because he philosophizes so much and the rhymes are confusing.

In the Passover holiday of that year, 1936, the Arabs once again attacked the Jewish community. Once again barricades of sandbags were set up on the eastern slope of the hill and this time there were about a dozen young men at the position. Either because they were so numerous or because times had changed, the men took great liberties. They cleared a space for themselves just below the tool shed, dragged planks from the corner of the yard, and set up a long table on which they ate their meals; they took hoes and picks without first obtaining permission and even bathed in the pool. The Abramovs kept quiet, but Alexander went out to the yard one morning, turned to the one who looked like a commander, and said that anyone who wanted to swim in the pool must first wash under the tap in the yard; and he also said that they were not to go up to the horses with pieces of bread and scraps of food.

"All right, boy," said the commander. "And it wouldn't hurt you to help fill the bags with sand."

Alexander replied that he had homework to do in the house and that when he had finished he would come and help. And he turned his back and went back to the house.

That evening a cellist and a viola player came from Tel Aviv and after dinner they sat down to play a quintet for two cellos. Apart from the strains of the music that carried through the open windows into the yard, the air also echoed with the sound of distant shots from the east and the faint sound of several blasts. The musicians looked up at each other while playing but from his armchair Abramov signaled to them to go on, and then, when they reached the climax of the second movement—in Alexander's opinion, in those days, the saddest and cruelest melody he had ever heard—Ingeborg set down the bow, let her violin fall from her hand to the floor, and said, "Enough, I can't go on, I want to go home," and she burst into tears.

Her husband and her son lifted her carefully from the chair and led her to her bedroom. This was not the first indication of her losing her wits. From time to time she would lie in bed for hours on end and refuse to get up or eat. Her silences would sometimes drag on for several days and then she would go back to the routine of everyday life filled up with few words and a smile that gradually became slightly frightening, growing more and more like a sort of perpetual soundless weeping.

The guests retreated to their rooms, Alexander was ordered to go to bed, and seventy-four-year-old Abramov sat at the bedside of thirty-six-year-old Ingeborg, held her hand, and whispered that she should try and sleep, that she should be calm, that everything would be all right, that they would soon go on a trip to Europe and she would be happy and healthy again. He heard her breathing become quiet and rhythmical and thought about the inevitable end approaching, about parting from this thing that was his life, the thing of which he strove to recall some substantial images but could not. It was as if Abram Alexandrovitch Abramov had never existed and in place of that man some scattered and disjointed incidents flickered in a vacuum, unconnected to each other. A wide river whose brown waters carried rafts made of hewn tree trunks; the loving face of a mother thanks to whom he was capable of sitting down at a piano to this very day; a dusky room in a wooden cabin containing a table with a green velvet cloth, a Russian woman serving tea and two submissive little girls watching him in awe from the corner, afraid to touch the bag of sweets he had brought them; and then complete darkness, the sound of a train drawing wagons to some unknown place in the night and the sound of words

coming up from beneath the window, the voices of youths in
the yard, strangers who had invaded his estate when he was
no longer capable of defending himself and driving them
away.

The youths' voices also reached Alexander's ears as he lay
awake in bed. If he could have been sure that his father
would not know and would not be angry, he would have got
up then, taken a rifle from the youths, and gone out to the
wadi to the east of the hill and shot at the Arabs and killed
them one after the other, despite all he had learned from
Michael Kohlhass. He would come upon them out of the
darkness and slay them, shoot and slay, kill and destroy those
guilty of all the evil that had befallen them.

8.

The final year at primary school drew to a close. In the
house Mother was lying in bed and a nurse was added to the
household, hired to tend the invalid. Father was spending
most of his time in his study, bent over ledgers or reading a
book. In the evening he would go down to the empty drawing
room and sit at the piano, start with one tune and pass on to
another, and sometimes he would play only accompaniments
and now and then stop and listen. Father and son ate their
meals alone, facing each other across the table and following
the maid with their eyes as she came and went with the food.

At the end of the summer holidays Alexander went to
Leah's house and told her that he was going to study at an
agricultural school. His mother's doctor had said that would
be better for him. The girl was not surprised because the
whole settlement already knew that Abramov's son was going
away and that his mother was mad. The girl held out both
hands to him, as if imploring him to take them in his, but
Alexander sat upright in his chair and looked into her eyes.

"I shall wait for you," said Leah, "even if it's forever."

"Forever?" said Alexander, perhaps mocking her, perhaps
thinking to himself, "There's no such thing as forever. Everything is much shorter."

After the holidays they loaded his belongings into the car

and his father drove him to the agricultural school in the north, about a hundred and twenty kilometers from their house on the hill. Boys who already been there a year or two and who were hanging around in the yard when the Abramovs arrived thought that Alexander had come accompanied by his grandfather; when they were told, some time later, that it was his father, it to some extent stopped them from recoiling from him because they took pity on him. The displeasure that he had aroused in these boys, even before he arrived, derived from their being aware that his parents were very rich and that they had thought of paying for a special room for their son, but the administration had not consented. Similarly they found ridiculous the luggage he had brought with him—a gigantic musical instrument in a black case and a record player with records.

Alexander placed the cello under his bed, and in order to do this he had to raise it with the help of bricks that he put under the four legs; he stood the record player on the little table by his bed, until there was no room for him to do his homework. Since his bed was now higher than the other beds in the room, there was an additional reason to see him as a braggart. With dizzying speed several painful things became clear to Alexander: that from now on he had to live with three strange and hostile boys, that if he did not want them to damage his cello and record player he would have to pacify or bribe them, and that if he did not want to add to his father's suffering his way home was barred.

For the first time in his life he would be forced to do things he did not feel like doing, ugly and degrading things, and before he decided to play this dishonorable game to the end, he resolved to hate them and take revenge on them when the time came. He did not know who he was going to hate and take revenge on and the obscurity enshrouding the object of his anger dismayed him even more.

Thus the gates to the next four years opened before him, and gritting his teeth, he swore furiously that he would withstand it, come what may.

Alexander felt some relief when he realized on the first evening—as he should have guessed from the start, had his anger not prevented him from thinking clearly—that the three other boys were strangers to each other, just as they were strangers to him. He introduced himself as Alex and learned that his roommates were called Nahman, Eli, and Uri; Uri and Eli came from the country and Nahman came from Tel Aviv. He had come to study agriculture because his mother was a socialist and she wanted her son to live by manual labor. Uri, from a settlement near Alexander's, retorted that it was possible to become bourgeois more quickly through agriculture than through trade. Eli was of the opinion that agriculture was hard work but satisfying. When it was Alexander's turn to explain, he said that his father had a farm but that he himself would be something else. He had not yet decided.

"And what do you want that instrument for?" Eli pointed to the cello under his bed. "You're living on the second floor because of it."

Alexander said that he played it.

"And what about this," persisted Eli, pointing to the record player, "doesn't this play?"

"That too," Alexander said briefly, and did not go on. There's a limit to cooperation with this idiot, he said to himself, but he remembered his resolution and continued, "If anyone has records that he wants to play, my record player is at your disposal; it's no problem."

Nahman said that they had records at home and that if he could he would bring some when he came back from the first holiday. As he said this he blushed.

Alexander brought a box of chocolates out of his case and offered it around.

"They're imported," said Eli. "That's what ruins our economy, foreign produce." And as he said this he took a piece for himself.

"So don't eat it," said Nahman of Tel Aviv. "No one's forcing you." Saying this, he blushed again and Alexander inwardly marked him up a point. He saw that Nahman did not blush with anger but with embarrassment, since it was obviously difficult for him to speak in front of strangers. Maybe he also felt bitter that he was being forced to live with people he did not know. Perhaps I can consider him.

Uri took a sweet and said thank you and nothing else. As he chewed the chocolate he chewed with gaping mouth, like a cow. At first Nahman refused to help himself but Alexander went on pressing him, and as Nahman put the sweet in his mouth, he turned his head slightly toward the wall, as if he did something that required modesty. He's possible, Alexander said to himself.

Before they all went to sleep Eli asked if Alex had a cigarette, and when told that he did not have one he turned his face to the wall and fell asleep at once. Uri said good night to those present before pulling the blanket over his head, and Nahman began to mumble something but changed his mind in the middle and lay on his back with his eyes shut, but it was obvious that he was not asleep. Alexander lay on his side with his back to the wall and his face toward the room. If he heard a noise in the night he would only have to open an eye in order to see if anyone meddled with his possessions.

Feeling that he would not be able to sleep, he soon sank into a heavy sleep, a dreamless sleep. When he awoke in the morning to the sound of a bell ringing, he opened his eyes and from his bed watched for a long time his friends' preparations for their first day; and when he finally realized that all this was not a nightmare but a new reality, he jumped out of bed and went to the shower. What are they doing there now, on the hill, he thought, and stamped his foot on the ground like a colt.

9.

The daily routine of the agricultural school—where the students rose at six in the morning at the sound of a bell and went to bed at lights-out at ten o'clock—made Alexander, after about a month, ready to believe that his whole life had proceeded along these lines for as long as he could remember. After a few months not only did discipline enter his daily life but also relationships with his friends. The fatigue he felt at the end of the day, which included work in the fields, deprived him of the leisure to remember and to daydream. Only the letters from his father took him back for a time to his past, but since one letter was very much like another, they gradually lost their power to plunge him into melancholy. His father would tell him again and again that there was no change in his mother's condition, that he himself carried on working as usual, and that he expected Alexander to make the most of his studies and he hoped that he was well.

Only his father's handwriting, clear and flowing at first, became a little untidy and at times it was difficult to decipher the words.

Nahman brought records from home and other boys also used his record player, but on Saturdays he was left alone in the room while the other boys were playing sport or strolling nearby, and then he would listen to the things that he had brought with him. On that day he would also pluck the cello and feel his touch gradually slipping away.

As the Passover holiday drew near, his father surprised him by coming to the school. His beard was longer, his face had grown long and thin, and his belly, which formerly indicated some muscular strength, had now fallen and sagged loosely in his trousers, which seemed to climb up to just under his chin.

His father had come to see him, of course, but also to tell him not to come home for the holiday. He brought Alexander a special present of money, with which he could spend the holiday in a hotel in the city if he wanted. His mother's condition was so poor, he said, that he didn't want Alexander to see her like that. She would doubtless improve in the future and then his father would let him know at once and would summon him to visit her.

Alexander did not ask his father to change his mind. They sat together in the dining hall for about an hour and drank tea. Alexander asked his father why he drove the car himself since it was a long and tiring journey.

"I dismissed the driver," said his father. "What do I want with a driver?"

Then they parted with a kiss.

From then on, the letters from home came less frequently, but near the end of the school year an unusually long letter arrived that again began by saying that there had been no improvement in his mother's condition, that his father was managing somehow, but that he had now decided to go to Europe for a while. He was leaving Alexander's mother in the capable hands of the nurse, and the doctor also visited her regularly. He had decided to travel because it might be better for his mother that way, and also because he wanted to see a few places before leaving them behind forever. Alexander was a big boy now and he knew that people did not live forever. Furthermore his father hoped that when he came back a miracle might happen and his mother might recover a little. Therefore there was no point in coming home for the holidays, and the money his son needed had already been sent to him by the bank, and when they'd meet again the following year, they would talk about everything calmly and at length.

Alexander applied for and received permission to stay at the school throughout the holiday. He would get his food from the caretakers who stayed there the whole year round.

10.

Alexander once more had a room to himself, and as soon as its occupants had vacated it, he tried to take up the cello again in the hope of a miracle. From now on he listened to records every day and wrote a lot in his diary.

There's shooting in the district again. The Arabs have declared a rebellion, or at least that's what they call it, and now they shoot both at us and at the English policemen. Every night here you can hear shots coming from the direction of the Bedouin. The name of their tribe is Zebe'h, but I don't think that they are taking part in the rebellion. It's not worth their while to take risks since they have flocks and crops here. I think that the shots come from the bands coming down from the Gilboa.

I play every day and listen to a lot of music. Now I've started to be really keen on Mozart. I didn't really pay him much attention before. He's probably the greatest of them all. I'm beginning to think so now.

Apparently my mother is finished and lately Father has also aged dreadfully. He has always been Father to me but last time I suddenly saw an old man. I am already fifteen and I must see things open-eyed. In fact, I have no choice. If I fall into howling it won't help at all.

Lately I have thought a lot about the three circles in

music. I can pierce the first circle the moment I read the notes, hum a bit to myself, or try something out on the piano. I get the idea and I am already inside the first circle. I pierce the second circle when I listen closely to the music or when I play it more or less correctly. Now comes the third circle. For what is music, in fact? It's speech. But the composer speaks not in words but in symbols, like a dumb man who talks with gestures and hopes that people understand him. He is not sure. He wants them to understand but he knows that signs get through only to someone who knows how to decipher them. This world that the composer tells about is a place, just as my room is a place, or my thoughts. It's usually a secret place belonging to the man himself. As a rule, people usually stand guard over a place like that and don't allow strangers to enter. But the composer is prepared to allow people to enter. The question is, just whom will he allow. I think only someone capable of piercing the third circle on his own. If the listener has the strength and intelligence to pierce through to the center of the music, that's a sign that the listener resembles the artist himself to some extent. Not that the listener is an artist but that he is capable of understanding and therefore he has permission to go inside. His entering will not disturb or mess up anything, but I think that this center is not only a secret place but also a dangerous place. It's a world so beautiful, so pure, that if you go inside you have two problems. First, how can you bear all that beauty and stay alive? And second, how will you manage to get out and carry on living in the ordinary world? I personally am probably not yet capable of entering, at least not on my own, but if I go in with someone else, then it would no longer be private. The whole thing would be ruined, and besides, who on earth might I go in with?

11.

Ten days or so after the beginning of the holiday, as he sat in his room and read a book, there was a knock on the door. The wife of the farm manager came into the room.

"I see that Mr. Abramov keeps to himself," she said, placing her hands on her thighs. "Don't you find it boring?"

The way she stood with her legs apart, the way she spoke, the broad smile on her face, the moist look in her eyes, the eyes of someone who is caught in a shameful act and who carries on smiling because he has no choice, made Alexander feel several things at once. First, he knew what she had come for, although he had never tried it; second, he would have liked to tell her to go to hell, because she had dared to enter his territory with the assumption that she had success already in her pocket; and third, he was hoping that she would not turn back. If she had turned her back on him now, he would have pounced on her from behind. But she did not, and after a little while, having turned the key and locked them in, she swooped and stripped off his clothes.

Alexander knew at that moment that he was betraying almost all the values that he had ordained to guide him through life. Her face was not beautiful, her hair was not clean, bristles of black hair sprouted around the nipples of her gigantic breasts, her pubic hair covered an alarmingly large area, five times what seemed fit to him; every one of her shameful movements made a lump of fat quiver on her enormous thighs, and her body exuded the smell of the sweat at the end of a day's work on the farm, the smell of a body long unwashed. Nevertheless he was drawn toward her as a sheaf of corn is borne in a tremendous storm, and as he penetrated her, he struck her flesh and bit the damp, greasy, slippery skin.

When he had finished, he moved away from her and sat up on the bed.

"Get dressed and go quickly, because your husband will kill you."

She started to gather up her clothes and he watched how

she stuck her thick legs into her drawers, which to his eyes looked as big as barley sacks.

"Lover boy," she said, her face suffused with a kind of delight that made him want to hit her, "I shall always come to you because we were good together."

"Don't you dare call me lover boy," screamed Alexander, "do you hear?"

His large eyes, which even now showed no anger but only that golden, unmoving fire, struck her with terror and she hastened to put on her blue overalls and leave the room.

12.

All night the sound of gunfire echoed around. Before the summer holidays, when the school had been full of boys, strict discipline had prevailed. In secret the students had trained with weapons, but not one of them was allowed to go out of bounds after nightfall. In the fields they worked under cover of guards. Now that Alexander had left on his own, he would slip out of the farm yard at dusk and wander around the plantations. He had to prove to himself that bands of murderers in the dark would not lay siege to him nor would they be able to scar his soul. On one occasion he tried to obtain a revolver from the gun closet but found it locked and so he went roaming empty-handed.

One evening, as he stood on the edge of the plantation and surveyed the slope that went down toward the Bedouin encampment at the other end of the wadi, a figure rose up out of the furrows of earth close to the scorched bushes, and a young Bedouin—about twenty years old—stood facing him at a distance of about four meters. For a moment they looked at each other in silence and then the Bedouin opened his mouth and with the foulest words, words used to speak to those despised and hated, he told Alexander that he was a son of a bitch and doomed to die, and that now his last moment had arrived, and before he killed him he was going to rape him and then he would bury him in the ground. The Bedouin grinned and called Alexander to come closer to him.

"I've been waiting here for you for three days, Jew," said

the Bedouin. "I swore to God that I would rape you and kill you like a dog. Come here you son of a whore, you won't get away from me."

Alexander made up his mind not to grant the Bedouin one single word. He examined the figure, trying to find out if his opponent had any weapons in his hands, but it seemed that the man stood before him empty-handed, barefoot, and wearing only his black rags. Alexander took one step forward and the Bedouin did the same. When they were standing about two meters apart, Alexander bent to the ground and grabbed a handful of earth; before he leaped forward, still in a crouching position, he threw the sand in the Bedouin's face. In the brief moment that he blinded his adversary Alexander jumped up and with his head rammed the man in the stomach.

The Bedouin, who had fallen backward, gripped Alexander by his hair and the two of them rolled on the ground, hitting each other, grabbing each other's clothes, pushing and hitting. Alexander noticed that the Bedouin was trying to reach out with his right hand for a dagger stuck in his belt and he could not manage to draw it. He freed himself momentarily from the man's body, and aiming a punch at his testicles with all his might, he dealt him a powerful blow in the lower part of his stomach. The cry of pain that burst from his throat, accompanied by a wailing groan, proved that he had scored a direct hit, and then Alexander jumped on his opponent, sat astride his chest, and seized his neck with both hands. He knew that the die had been cast.

Alexander bent over the Bedouin's face in order to increase the pressure of his hands, and he felt how his fingers and nails were stuck between the neck muscles, touching the artery and tearing the skin. His hands continued to press down, and he heard a faint choking sound and suddenly noticed a smell that he had not noticed all that time.

It was a smell from the man's clothes, his body and hair. The smell of the smoke of an Arab stove that burned dung, the smell that used to fill the courtyard of their house at sunset in the days of his childhood, when the Arab workers left their work to go and bake bread and sit down to their meal. Unbeknown to his mother, he would be given pieces of warm pita by the workers, and as he ate it hungrily, he felt grains of sand being ground between his teeth.

Alexander saw before him bulging eyes, a swarthy face, and a final redness draining away from beneath the graying skin. Now the body twitched under him, as if wanting to be embraced and surrender. Between his knees the Bedouin's ribs sank to the earth and Alexander knew that what had been done could not be undone. Now only the smell remained, and all around there was a sudden stillness; and out of the stillness, from far off, there came the sound of dogs barking and some indistinct bleating, or perhaps the sound of a bird. Alexander let go of the man's neck. His fingers were seized by spasms and he shook them, straightening and bending them until they became flexible again. He was still sitting on the dead man's chest and he brushed the sand off his victim's face, closed his eyes, and considered the face, both strange and familiar at the same time, and he got to his feet. Stumbling, almost crawling on all fours, he made his way to the tool shed of the plantation and came back with a shovel in his hands. He dragged the body between the trees, dug a pit, and buried the dead man in it, taking care to spread dry earth over the grave. In order to blur his tracks Alexander waded a few hundred meters along an irrigation ditch full of water, got out onto the road, and from there he went back to the farmyard.

Back in his room he took a shower, changed his clothes, and lay on his bed until morning. At half-past five he was on the road and took the first bus to Haifa. He left a note in the school office saying that he had had to go home to visit his sick mother.

As he sat in the bus he saw in his mind's eye what would be happening in the school now. The Bedouin would have informed the police of the youth's disappearance. Dogs would have been brought in and would have discovered the corpse and the police would have arrested the farm manager and taken him for questioning. The man would have managed to establish an alibi without any difficulty, and since there had been no one but him in the school, the farm manager would have realized that Alexander's journey was connected with the murder.

13.

As he went through the gate of the yard, his suitcase in one hand and the cello in the other, he saw the nurse standing by a bed with an awning over it, in the shade of the wall, and she was pouring tea. In the bed, on raised pillows, lay his mother, and he saw the profile of her face, which had become sharp and shriveled and only her large eyes remained of what he remembered of her. He went up to the bed, looked at his mother, but did not manage to catch her eye. She looked straight ahead, her hands resting on the sheet on either side of her.

"Mutti," he said in German, "Mother, I've come to see you."

Ingeborg turned to look at him and a long time went by before she replied.

"You went off on your own to Zurich," she said, "and you left me here. . . . Now go and pack the bags; they are waiting for me. . . . The rehearsals have already started and you are doing nothing. . . . Go, go quickly and pack the cases. . . . I'm ready."

At a distance, near the tool shed, Alexander saw the Jewish foreman and his two laborers watching him with curiosity. When he raised his head and looked at them, they busied themselves with their work again and turned to face the orchard.

"Mutti," he said, "you have to get better and then we shall all travel."

"Where is that man?" Ingeborg whispered in sudden terror. "He mustn't know, Alexis . . . he mustn't know anything. . . . Just the two of us will get away from here now . . . before he comes back."

The nurse told him that his mother had better times when she would read a book, eat well, and even smile, but most of the time she was the way he saw her. The doctor had not gven up hope.

Alexander went into the house, saw that the furniture was wrapped in white sheets, and a chill smell of mildew lingered in the rooms despite the summer heat outside. His father's study was locked and apparently Abramov had taken all the keys with him when he went to Europe. He was supposed to return in the autumn. In his own room Alexander found a bed stripped of bedding, a vase without flowers, and the carpet rolled up and tucked under the desk. From the window of the room came the sound of the motor and the pool being filled with water in preparation for the day when they watered the orchard.

He went back to the courtyard. His mother lay under the awning, with her eyes closed, and the nurse asked him when he would want to eat and how long he would be staying at the house. He answered that he would not be going back to school until the beginning of the term in the autumn.

He went down the hill to Leah's house. The girl did not know what to do when Alexander appeared before her, and since he did not hug her and carried on talking to her as if they had parted only yesterday, she burst into tears. Then he took her hand and stroked it.

"Come on," he said. "We'll go for a little walk."

He noticed the changes that had occurred in Leah and was agitated, but he showed no signs of surprise. The girl he had left a year ago was now a woman in every way, and in many respects her body had developed completely new features, not unlike those he had seen in the farm manager's wife, but infinitely more lovely.

They skirted the hill with his house from the east and went into the orchard at the point where the well house stood. There an iron pipe carried water from the motor to the pool and part of the pipe was supported in the air at head height. Alexander climbed onto the pipe and started to walk along it like a tightrope walker while Leah walked close by on the ground.

"It's not difficult when you get used to it," he told her. "Do you want to try it?"

Leah did not want to and gave an embarrassed laugh. She would have preferred him to walk at her side and hold her hand, but he insisted upon completing the prank and walking along the pipe until the place where it went back into the ground. Then he paused a moment, looked at the black cylinder lying on the clods of loose earth, kicked the pipe, and said, "You ought to know that I have kept the promise I made you. I have already avenged your father's blood . . . last night. That's why I came to you, to let you know."

Leah did not dare ask and waited for him to go on and explain, but Alexander remained silent and they walked between the trees, up the hill toward the house.

Then he added, "I can't reveal the details to you, but believe me, I really did it and now I have to stay here in the settlement until the end of the holidays because I'm hiding from the police."

She was frightened and suggested that he should stay in her mother's house because they would certainly not look for him there. Alexander replied that he had carried out the operation very carefully, even perfectly, and that the police had no chance of tracking him down.

When they reached the house, he ordered the nurse to serve a meal for two and he dined with Leah in the kitchen. Throughout the meal he did not take his eyes off the innovations in his childhood girlfriend.

As if reading his thoughts, the girl said to him, blushing and smiling, "You've changed so much, Alex. . . . You're awfully handsome now, even more than you were before. I just thought that you would like to know."

"I've kept the promise I gave you," said Alexander. "Now I don't owe anyone anything."

Lately he had resolved that he would never marry. The farm manager's wife was conclusive evidence of what they were capable of, these women. Then he looked into Leah's eyes to see whether she had understood what he said to her, but what he saw in her eyes filled his heart with weariness and despair. Her eyes were a mixture of supplication, affection, and surrender. Why did she not run for her life? Why did she not take offense and slam the door behind her? Had she done that, he might have gone to see her the following day, but she still sat opposite him, swamped him with a look of dumb devotion, her breasts rising and falling and her fingers fidgeting with the tablecloth.

"I didn't sleep all night," said Alexander. "I'll take you home and then go to sleep."

She quickly assured him that there was no need to take her home, that he should rest as much as he needed, and that they would meet again the next day. And she rose from the table, kissed him on the cheek, and made her way out of the room, while he followed the rippling of her thighs under her light summer dress. Then he gave a long yawn and went to his room.

14.

In the mornings Alexander would stay with his mother, waiting for her to shrivel up and disappear before his eyes. After such an encounter he needed a long walk in the orchard before he could think of playing his cello. Then he would head for the library in the house, once again taking out the books that had seemed so important to him two or three years before, and he read them again. After lunch he would make another attempt to engage his mother in conversation and sometimes he would hear his name on her lips again. Until late in the afternoon he lay on his bed, fast asleep with a book in his hand, and woke up at dusk. Then Leah would come up the hill, carrying with her a jar of red sabra juice, boiled with sugar, that her mother had made, and they would sit on the balcony and talk to each other. Leah was going to study at a teachers' training college when she left secondary school. Alexander had not decided what he would do, but it was now clear to him that he would not be a cellist, although he would continue to play for pleasure. He might go and study engineering at the Institute of Technology in Haifa, or he might be a ship's captain. If he were not dependent upon his father's will he would go on board right now and sail off to faraway countries.

After dinner they would go up to his room and lock the door. As early as his second day at home Leah had told him that she was his wife, from now to eternity, and as for his not wanting to get married at all, it did not mean anything; when he became a man and would "find out about life," he would change his mind. She was prepared to wait and she would not love anyone but him, that was something that could not be changed. Alexander told her that she was taking on a "heavy responsibility," since in his opinion he was not capable of "truly loving" anyone and he would always want to roam around the world and had no desire whatsoever to raise a family and have children. He wanted to be as free as the birds and beasts, and as far as friendship was concerned, he had two friends—music and books. It would be better for Leah to think about this while there was still time left and find herself a "suitable man." It was true that he was very fond of her, "but that was pure chance" and one should not depend on chance.

She repeated that she was sure that the future held other solutions in store and that, meanwhile, there was no one in the world for them except each other; she belonged to him, and whether he knew it or not, he belonged to her. Then she would no longer hesitate but would hold him tightly, stroke his face, covering him with kisses and trembling with excitement. When he tried to lift her skirt, she said that they would do that later, when they were really man and wife, and meanwhile, would he please not take off her clothes because she wanted him with all her heart and she would end up giving in to him, and then where would they be? So it was agreed that they would lie in his bed with their clothes on, but so that her dress would not crease and so that her mother would not know anything, it was agreed that she would take off her clothes—while Alexander turned his face to the wall—and she would put on a lace petticoat that Alexander brought from his mother's wardrobe. They used to lie in bed like that, he in a shirt and summer shorts and she in the lace petticoat, which was too long for her and completely transparent, but constituted a barrier between the present and the day when things would be different and the restriction would be lifted.

Nearly swooning with happiness, she would lie in his arms, trembling, her eyes closed and her mouth and hands exploring his body. Alexander would run his hands over his mother's petticoat, and when he came to certain places, Leah would flinch, catch his hand, kiss it, and ask him to forgive her for making him suffer so much although she wanted only to give him happiness and love. Her eyes were always closed and his eyes were always wide open. At times the twitching of her body reminded him of the twilight hour he spent in the school plantation with the young Bedouin, but most of the time he would look at her face with his eyes closed until he no longer saw her and in her place came some unknown figure, reminding him of something dim, yet almost familiar.

This image would come out of a forest that Alexander would reach on his travels around the world; or she would appear to him on a street corner at night, when he was returning from a concert or a cabaret in one of the cities his father had told him about; sometimes he ran into her in Zurich or Munich. And he was never surprised, for he had been waiting for her for such a long time that her appearance was more the fulfillment of a promise than a surprise. And then the image would fade again and there was Leah lying in his arms, the girl who lived down in the settlement at the bottom of the hill among the people about whom his father and mother and their Arab cook had warned him, a long time ago. Those happy days were so remote that he could have cried out in anger, and Leah, in his arms, lay at the center of this anger; she was not guilty, she had not done anything wrong, she merely symbolized and exemplified the terrible wrong done to him.

15.

His father returned home a few days before the end of the summer holidays. He spoke now with a permanent rattle that came from deep in his throat, and his beard had grown long and almost completely white. All his life Alexander had seen his father as a burly Russian, one of those landowners whose pictures he had seen in anthologies of Russian literature; now he saw him as a sort of Jewish rabbi in whose wounded look it was difficult to tell whether there lay implacable anger or awesome compassion. He embraced Alexander and held him for a long time; he did not ask why his son had come even though several months earlier he had urged him not to come here; he went alone to Ingeborg's room and stayed there until darkness fell, and in the evening the two of them sat at the dining table and the father said to his son, "So, you see, I've come home."

A few days later Alexander went back to school.

The headmaster called him to his room and questioned him for a long time about the reason for his sudden journey home, but Alexander stubbornly insisted that he had had to go and see his sick mother.

After a few days everyone was talking about the corpse of the Bedouin found buried in the plantation and about the arrest of the farm manager, who had denied any connection with the matter and had been set free. A few weeks later everyone was sure that Alexander had murdered the Bedouin and he became the hero of all the pupils. Eli, his roommate, said explicitly, "Good job," while Uri urged him to tell the truth down to the minutest detail, as was usual between friends. To this Nahman commented that there were some things that you don't talk about even between friends. Upon hearing these words Alexander decided that one of these days he might tell Nahman everything.

Toward the end of the second year the boys were organized class by class in military order after having taken the oath on the rifle and Bible as members of the Haganah organization. Alexander was appointed a section commander and during the first vacation he was sent on a sabotage course at a kibbutz near Haifa. At the end of the course he went home for two days. He found no change in his mother's condition and his father would talk to himself and finish with a wave of his hand, as if he were driving away a fly. On the night that he spent in the house Leah came to his room and put on his mother's petticoat, and he told her that he had now decided to become a soldier, and when a Jewish state arose he would be a general.

At the end of the third school year the Second World War broke out. Refugee ships tried to break through the blockade on their way from Europe to Palestine, but the British army opened fire on them and their passengers were sent to concentration camps. The passengers of one ship committed suicide in Haifa harbor and another ship hit a mine and its passengers drowned. The Haganah organization called upon its members to fight the British and at the same time to volunteer for the British army in order to fight Hitler.

"It can't possibly work like that," Alexander said to Nahman. "They should make up their minds. Either we fight the British or we join the British army and fight Hitler "

To this Nahman answered, "We will fight the British as if there were no Hitler, and we will fight Hitler as if the British were not our enemies. That's what one of the leaders says."

"Well, you can tell the leader that in that case we night as well all march off to the lunatic asylum," said Alexander. "As for me, it's quite simple; I shall fight the British."

Alexander soon found his way into the ranks of an underground splinter movement and was expelled from school.

After about two and a half years, when Rommel's army was threatening to conquer Egypt and Palestine, Alexander rejoined the Haganah. He went to one of the commando units in the Galilee in order to "stop the German army and make it possible for the Australians to retreat to Syria," according to the commanders, one of whom was Nahman. He heard from him that Uri had been killed in a bridge-blowing operation and Eli had lost both legs in the same operation.

When Rommel was repulsed from the Western Desert, Alexander took a holiday and went home. On arrival he found his father sitting at the piano and wearing a woolen robe, but not playing. He asked after his mother and his father told him in a hushed voice that her condition had considerably improved, but just at that time she had committed suicide, having hoarded the medicines she had been given and swallowing them all at once. And after saying this, he passed his left arm over the keys, from left to right, and he finished off by vigorously striking the lowest key with a finger of his right hand. Then he silently and carefully closed the lid of the piano and said, "Well, that's how it is," and lifting his eyes to Alexander, he added, "That's how it is, my dear Sasha. You are bereft of a mother and soon you will lose your father. How old are you now? Twenty-one? Well, when I was your age I had finished at the Polytechnic, and what about you? Think about it, Sasha. Think carefully."

In the night Leah came to his room, refused to put on his mother's petticoat, and as she got into bed naked with him, she said that from then on she would be both a mother and a wife to him. "You can cry, Alex," she told him. "Even a man like you is allowed to cry for Mother. Don't be embarrassed, my love. . . . There, hold me and cry a little."

"Only women," said Alexander, "shed tears. And they cry

so much that it sometimes seems to me that they enjoy it. With men, tears are reserved for other matters."

"Which matters, Alex?"

"Music and tales. You wouldn't understand, nor is there any need for you to understand."

She was not offended. In fact, she felt like laughing at the theory she had just heard, but she refrained on account of the solemnity of the occasion. She buried her head in her lover's splendid chest and renounced her virginity to the boy who, in her opinion, did not realize how distressed he should have been on that day.

16.

During the last two years of the world war Alexander shifted from one military course to another. In between he prepared for his matriculation in order to be able to study at the Institute of Technology. He learned how to assemble and dismantle mines, and as a result, he began to think that he might like to study chemistry. He thought mainly about the invention of weapons that could be used in the final struggle to rid the country of the British.

He traveled a lot from place to place, staying in flats belonging to the underground, and from time to time he joined units journeying in the Judean Desert or the Negev. Prolonged and exhausting marches and extreme weariness were a sort of compulsion for him, but at the end of a long day he could not sleep and would sit in the opening of the reconnaissance tent, smoking a cigarette and gazing into the darkness. At times the strains of a string quartet came to him and sometimes he felt that a face he had already seen before was looking at him out of the darkness, and then he would say to himself that he was closer than ever to meeting that face. At times he would remember his cello and wonder why he was on the road instead of sitting in his room on the hill and playing; and when he finally went to bed in the tent, he would think about Leah and resolve that the next time he would point out to her the embarrassing mistake and make her understand once and for all that she had to forget him.

The poor girl deserved to be treated honestly, he would reproach himself. I must finish it once and for all. He would lie there and with his eyes closed until morning, occasionally sinking into a short sleep and waking up again with a shudder.

When he returned from a trip like this, he would sleep solidly for two days. And then he would go back to the courses and to the journeying and the minor military operations that harassed the lives of the British soldiers and police.

When he was twenty-four he started studying at the Institute of Technology, but even in the very first year his studies were interrupted by operations in which he took part and by a three-month journey to Italy as a member of a buying delegation for the underground. In those days he was quite an expert on materials needed for sabotage and his mastery of languages made him extremely useful in doing business with arms dealers.

In 1948, when he was twenty-six and had already managed to abandon his chemisty studies in favor of mechanical engineering, the British left Palestine and the War of Independence began. Then he left the Institute of Technology for good and became an officer in the army that was set up in the course of a few weeks.

17.

About three years after the end of the War of Independence, Alexander was still serving in the army, but even then he wandered from unit to unit, traveled frequently to Europe to buy arms, and he spent the greater part of 1952 journeying. In London he received a telegram from Nahman, at that time an officer in the General Staff and directly responsible for Alexander, that said that his father was dying.

He found the ninety-year-old Abramov lying in the double bed in his bedroom, breathing heavily and stroking the pillow that had been Ingeborg's.

Did he really love her? Alexander asked himself. At this thought his heart was filled with sudden joy that took him so much by surprise that he bent over his father and kissed him on the forehead, stroked his face, and whispered to him words he used to utter more than twenty years before, in the days when they were both absorbed in reading a Russian fairy tale or just before he went to sleep, when his father would shut the book on his knees and tuck in the blanket around Alexander's body, and then, sometimes, he would dare to whisper, "I love you, Father," and his father would smile at him, put his finger to his lips, and leave the room.

Did he really love her? If that was really the case, it meant that that possibility was immersed even in Alexander's blood; it might then surface and burst into his life before he was ninety. His hand still lay on his father's cold moist brow and he did not want to remove it until the last moment. It was probably a foolish idea that had occurred to him, but he was captivated by it and refused to part from it; in Alexander's hand there coursed his mother's blood and maybe as he touched his father he was giving the dying man the greatest of presents—her forgiveness, the touch of her flesh on his, the thing his father was trying to find in the pillow at his side, upon which his hand had ceased to move.

18.

When he saw just how neglected the family assets had been, Alexander left the army and went back to live in the house he had left sixteen years before, when he was fourteen.

Alexander Abramov was thirty when he came to inherit the estate that he had never taken part in running. He was surprised that a man of ninety could govern, in no uncertain way, the Jewish foreman, his socialist laborers, and the crisis that had befallen the citrus business during the war. The confusion in the ledgers prevented him from forming any picture of the situation and he approached matters in the only way he knew: He dismissed all the laborers and hired a few shift workers to look after the trees, and then he sat in his father's study and waited for the bills to come from the creditors, the electric company, the fertilizer suppliers, the marketing company, and the cooperative. Meanwhile, he rummaged through the drawers of the desk and the shelves, found a photograph album from his mother's childhood days and a thick file with his father's diploma in forestry and Russian deeds for forest lands with contracts of sale and purchase from the beginning of the century all folded up inside. He put the library in order, separated the scores from the books, arranged them by language, and carried bundles to the window and shook the dust and cobwebs off them. In order to break into the iron strong box, for which the keys could not be found, he called in a locksmith from the settlement. In the box he found a small fortune in English, Russian, and Austrian gold coins, accounts that he could not decipher, and his parents' marriage certificate.

Meanwhile, the bills started arriving, and when he added them up, it became perfectly clear to him that if he wanted his estate to run on firm foundations he would have to sell off about ten acres out of his sixty acres.

On the western side of the hill the settlement stretched out, just as in his childhood, and on the eastern side new housing estates had sprung up, where immigrants from Yemen, Hungary, and North Africa lived. Alexander decided to sell ten acres on the side of the eastern slope, so that on the side of the old settlement the distance between him and it would not lessen.

Leah was living alone in the house she had inherited from her mother, and she was teaching in the school where they had both studied in their childhood. Several of the teachers had suggested more than once, at their meetings, that they should fire her because she was "a bad example to the pupils," because she was the common-law wife of the officer, the heir to the estate on the hill; but the parents' committee defended her. The farmers were still sure that one of these days the teacher would be the mistress of the big house, to which none of them had had access since the day it was built.

When he had a clear idea of the state of the farm, Alexander told Leah about his decision to sell ten acres on the eastern slope. Leah saw his eyes, through the smoke from the pipe in his mouth, and guessed that his heart was breaking at the thought of being separated from the land hitherto so highly prized. She guessed that if this wall were broken through, Alex would be miserable and would never forgive.

And who, if not Leah herself, would pay the price of the anger that would fill his heart?

"I have a proposal to make, Alex," she said, and her heart beat within her chest as it had on the day when they kissed each other for the first time. "You must not sell any part of the estate. . . . We can sell my house and the land beside it. In any case, I'm not capable of looking after a farm and my tenant is doing me out of more and more each year."

Leah was thirty years old when she sealed her fate with her own hands. She was in her prime and Alexander knew that nature would not bestow on her any more than it already had. The women he had known in army camps—the little secretaries who leaped into the officers' camp beds; the women he had been with on his travels in Europe, in hotel rooms; the ripe wives of his acquaintances on the staff who lusted after his youth and pitted their charms against his cool and aloof character—all these seemed like things that had happened not to him but to someone else. With polite and well-concealed impatience he would wait for them to get out of his bed and go back to where they belonged. Only Leah's presence did not disturb his composure because when he was with her, from the very moment she came to him, another figure, an incorporeal being that hovered over him, would come out of its hiding place, approaching him and withdrawing, leaving him with the promise of a further appearance.

They took their marriage vows at the end of the winter.

19.

The economic recovery of the estate on the hill was thought to take a long time, and Alexander put a detailed proposal to Nahman that he should serve as a supplier of spare parts for tank and airplane engines. His connections abroad were good, and Nahman, then one of the assistants of the minister of defense, had no reason to refuse. Only a formal screening remained to be carried out, and Alexander's file was handed to three people—a psychologist, an accountant, and a staff officer in the intelligence—who were all asked to present a report before his wish would be granted.

Alexander, son of Abram Abramov, thirty years old; mother a German Christian who did not convert. Height: 189 centimeters, athletic build, brown hair, light brown eyes, healthy with no hereditary illnesses. (The illness of his mother, who committed suicide in 1943, was explained by the doctor as depression without genetic cause springing from the age difference—36 years—between her and her husband and from the isolation in which she lived, separated from local society.) Military career: positive, rank of major. Education: technical with no academic degree. One year in a dissident underground group (1941–42). Owner of agricultural property valued at one and a half million Israeli pounds, in bad condition but with prospects of recovery. He has sums of about eighteen thousand Israeli pounds available in ready cash. He was married a month ago to a teacher in a primary school. Background: farmer's daughter, served in the Haganah. Stable character. Her property was sold before her marriage to pay off the debts of her husband's estate.

Description of character, behavior, and habits: good-looking and aloof. On no occasion has he been known to mislead. Usually gives balanced and realistic reports. Estimated ability to resist interrogation under torture: excellent. In the 1948 campaign he displayed courage, composure, and devotion to friends in trouble. He was decorated for saving a wounded friend under fire in Iraq-Souedan.

Prefers solitude and does not make friends easily. He has no background in a youth movement, apart from membership in the Haganah when he was studying at an agricultural school (1937–41). Good leadership ability, without clear ambition for a military career. Son of rich parents, which accustomed him, from childhood, to keeping his distance. Dresses very smartly. In the last two years he has bought all his civilian suits abroad, when traveling on army and defense ministry business. General appearance English, not unintentionally. He has an inner need to maintain a distinct outward reserve toward his surroundings. This reserve enables him to show complete loyalty to the cause in hand, but he feels obliged to conceal this loyalty in order to preserve a sort of capricious, almost childish freedom. He is a quintessential romantic vis-à-vis concept of integrity, honor, and loyalty, but as a counterbalance to romanticism he has a well-developed sense of reality and astuteness. This does not make life any easier for him, but makes him eminently suitable and extremely well qualified for intelligence duties and for missions demanding devotion, secrecy, and daring.

To conclude: recommended for any category of classified mission. A successful combination of character, which will not betray, and property, which will prevent him from being tempted by embezzlement. No reservations.

When Nahman finished reading the document, he said to his adjutant, "I don't know why I hold psychologists in so much disdain. Here, look what these idiots have written this time. The description of Alex is one hundred percent on target and I have known the fellow since the age of fourteen. I wouldn't have been able to give a more precise description; there's only one thing they didn't notice: the melancholy, the willingness to forfeit his life, the flirtation he conducts with death. I hope that there'll be a change in him now that he's married. A miserable chap, all in all."

It was agreed that Alexander would bring tenders for spare parts and ammunition from three countries, and he flew to western Europe with Leah. This was her first time away from home, and Alexander devoted their first three days in London to shopping for her. When she was weighed down with sets of clothing, shoes, handbags, bottles of perfume, and packets of tea and chocolates, he turned to his business and advised her to stroll around the city and enjoy herself.

20.

When they returned from their journey, Alexander rented two rooms in Tel Aviv and set up his office there. The tenders he had brought back were well received; several of the military attachés in Israeli embassies in Europe were ex-comrades-in-arms and had fond recollections of him and helped him along; he left the affairs of the estate in the hands of a demobilized officer, one of his friends from the agricultural school.

At first he would go home every evening, but gradually his stays in Tel Aviv became more lengthy and Leah raised no objection to this. He moved his cello and many records to the office and one of the rooms became a second home to him. He rarely played the cello but he listened to the records nearly every evening that he did not go home. He used to meet his business acquaintances in restaurants and cafés. No one was invited to his office outside working hours.

In the house on the hill Leah was free to make her own arrangements. She bought a brush and paints and in the course of two weeks she painted, with her own hands, the walls of the drawing room, the bedrooms, the study, and the library. She did not touch the outside walls since the reddish color of the plaster had not faded and still retained its cheerful freshness, which blended so well with the lush green of the trees in the orchard around the house, a garden of pomegranates, figs, and a giant Dabuki vine that in the summer cast a shadow over an area of about a quarter of an acre.

The maid helped her to remove the paint stains from the floor, and when the rooms once more shone in their bluish white, Leah turned her attention to the wardrobes. She looked for Ingeborg's petticoat and found it, the transparent lace petticoat, and hid it in a cardboard box at the bottom of the wardrobe after she had placed between its folds twigs of thyme, myrtle, and marjoram leaves that she had collected in the orchard.

In the autumn a son was born to them and during the next three years two daughters were born.

Alexander spent the first three years of marriage in numerous journeys to Europe and from each one he would bring his wife dresses, sweaters, shoes, and perfumes even though she had urged him to desist, since the house was becoming like a clothes warehouse to last her for the rest of her life. At the end of every journey he would stay on the hill for a few days and then go back to his office in Tel Aviv, where he now spent weeks on end without visiting the settlement.

In the fifth year of their marriage Leah went back to her job in the school and within a short time she was occupied with meetings of the Cultural Committee, the Soldiers' Welfare Committee, the local branch of the Women's Movement, and the Southern Regional Folk Choir. The estate on the hill prospered once more and two women lived in the house with Leah, one to take care of the housework and the other to look after the children.

At night, which she spent alone in her enormous empty house, she started studying for a degree in education; if it was not too late she would telephone Alexander to hear his voice and tell about the children and relate what they had said that day. She did not dare to call him late at night lest he think that she was spying on him. With her eyes wide open she would lie on her double bed and tell herself for the thousandth time that she had no right to complain, because no one had misled her. Alex had never lied to her and she would never do or say anything that would make him lie to her.

When their son was six and went to the same school at which his father had arrived one autumn morning thirty-one years before, the child knew that his mother was close by, in one of the nearby classrooms, and he fled to her on the very first day when children of eight and nine asked him if he really had a father and where his father was.

When their son was ten, the school psychiatrist advised them to transfer him to a boarding school away from home, because the father's continuous absence from home, and especially his sudden visits, confused the boy and made him nervous and aggressive. It would be better for him to live at boarding school, where he would have a regular and unchanging routine. Stability was more necessary to him now than his mother's proximity, which was no longer enough. So he was sent to a boarding school reputed to have a modern, skilled, and experienced psychologist.

21.

Alexander worked as a supplier of spare parts and ammunition for only three years before becoming completely fed up with it. The estate started to bring in profits and to his surprise he realized that in these few years he had earned sums of money in his arms deals to suffice him for many years. What was he to turn to now, and what should he do with his life? It had not become burdensome to him, for he had filled it with journeys, surrounded himself with great luxury, played a little, and listened a lot to concerts and records; but apart from music, he had not known happiness, and the joy that music brought him was more like torment than pleasure.

Today I have decided to close another circle. I am selling my company and going back to the regular army, if they will have me. I need more movement and tension than I can get from business. The continual proximity to the house in the settlement and my continuous absence from it burden me with a feeling of humiliation. Evening after evening I know that I should be there, but I stay here. If my work were to be entirely or mainly abroad, it would be easier for me.

I must also be closer to the cities my father told me about, because in one of these cities I shall meet her. Lately she has almost been shouting, "Unless you reach out your arms I shall also keep away from you."

My theory about the three circles of music does not of course have any objective validity, and if I were to submit it to the academy, they would scoff at it, quite rightly; but it has lost none of its validity in my inner world, which perhaps resembles more and more the world surrounding my mother before her death. It's a fact that lately I have been piercing the inner circle, and I am not alone there. The girl, or the woman, with the

dark copper hair and dark honey eyes, is waiting for me
inside the third circle; and I don't understand—each
time, anew, I don't understand—how I come out of
there and return to reality, alive and sane.

I have decided to sell the company and go back to the
army. If they will not accept my conditions I shall think
about something else.

Alexander sold his business and informed the Ministry of
Defense that he wanted to work as a regular officer in one
of the intelligence services, that his experience and knowledge of languages fitted him for work abroad, and that from a
material point of view he was independent and had no interest in commerce and profits.

At first he was taken into the Arabic section, and when another war broke out between Israel and her neighbors, in
1956, he was praised glowingly for his success in interrogating prisoners and collecting intelligence material. What surprised him was the intense yearning he felt whenever he was
about to come into contact with an Arab prisoner or with an
informant from the Arab armies. At every one of these meetings there hovered—in the atmosphere of the interrogation
room, or in the darkness that shrouded the meetings in the
fields and the wadis—the figure of the Bedouin youth with
whom he had struggled in the plantation in Galilee. It was as
if the youth had returned to life and it became once more
possible to bring back and reconstruct, retrospectively, what
might have happened, had everything been different.

The Arabs brought to him for investigation did not
threaten to murder or rape him, but he knew that they would
have cheerfully killed him if they could have done so; and as
he talked to them, without touching them, he could trace the
terror, the shame and the despair in their souls, the same terror that—under different circumstances—would pass over
into their bodies and make them give a last terrifying spasm,
with only a small difference between it and a final desire, a
desire in which bodies unite, souls meet and become one, in
some distant, mysterious plain.

These Arabs that I, in fact, persecute because they have
fallen into my hands, handcuffed and beaten, who are

they if not those same Arab laborers in the yards of our house; those same Arabs with whom I chased hares; those same Arabs whose working mothers would catch me secretly in the shed and cover my face with kisses; the first woman from whom I heard, when I was six, that I was handsome, that they wanted to kidnap me and take me home with them. Now I sit their sons down facing an electric light and repay them with mortal fears in return for the childhood joys I knew with them and for their mothers' love.

I'm not apologizing. They regard us with deadly hatred and I'm just doing what is possible and necessary to do. But this does not alter the fact that in return for the friendship of one Arab I would give ten American, English, or French friends. With a European I can drink whiskey, do business, and come to an understanding that the state of Israel is in fact an extension of Europe in the east; but with an Arab I can once again roll about in the clods of earth in the plantation, inhale the smell of an oven burning goat dung, pick and eat thyme, run toward the horizon and find my childhood there, and perhaps also find a point to life—now almost aimless— within the place where the hill of my childhood stands.

22.

About a year later, Alexander was transferred abroad and he stayed there for about twelve years, returning to Israel several times a year, as much as was necessary for his work. He divided his stay in Israel between the department that employed him and the house on the hill. On one of these visits he learned of the psychologist's advice to send his son away from home.

My father did the same to me in his old age, when he was a beaten and desperate man and had a wife at home who lay dying in his arms for six years. But I am doing it to my son while my wife is sane and biting her lips in order not to scream with fear and anger; I am the madman, and behind the upholstered and luxurious madness there lurks a father who allows his son to be dragged away and bound up ready for sacrifice. I can't turn the wheel back, and even if I could, what would we be going back to? I'm not sure that my son will be pleased when he hears them tell him one day, "Your father wanted to die and thus he did not know how to live." If my son is sane and sensible he will say, "Then why didn't he die a long time ago, before he begot me?"

Sometimes during his stays in Israel he would be asked to help to interrogate suspects, and on one occasion a Greek man was brought before him, a doctor of something to do with the history of the Mediterranean. The man was suspected of having links with a Greek priest who aided Arab terrorists. It was an unfounded suspicion, but from the conversation with the man some memories lingered in Alexander's mind—partly pleasant, partly bitter—because the Greek had spoken about the revival of the Mediterranean peoples and about an ancient culture soon to come back to life; the Greek also said that in the evening he was going to listen to Mozart quartets, and Alexander suddenly longed to take off his dark glasses and the fatuous disguise of mustache and beard he wore during the interrogation and to say to the Greek, "Come on, let's go together and then you can tell me more about the Mediterranean revival." But instead of this he voiced threats in the Greek's ears, told him that they would have their revenge on the priest if he did not reveal his connections with him; and only when they parted did Alexander abandon his restraint and shake hands with the man he had been interrogating. The dark glasses and the disguise had helped him to overextend himself a little.

About twelve years later, when he met the same Greek again, he regretted not having shot him dead on their first meeting; on their second meeting he had to forgo this pleasure, since Alexander was no longer what formerly he had been.

And meanwhile, he went back to his journeyings and homecomings, to the records in hotel rooms in Europe, and to the two little girls who became more and more terrified whenever he tried to hug them, and to the wife who had be-

come a stranger, plump and looking hard and exhausted, the
wife who had shouldered the enormous old family house—
the house upon which the people of the settlement were now
taking their revenge. They refused to come to it even when
the mistress of the house tried to invite her friends from different organizations to hold their meetings there.

23.

In 1967 the Israelis conquered the whole of the West Bank of
the Jordan, including the Old City of Jerusalem. Although he
was very busy with his journeys, Alexander tried to stay in Israel as much as he could that year. He would journey to the
conquered territories and go right out to the Arab villages
where time stood still. He would enter into conversations with
men sitting in the coffeehouses of the villages, listening to and
telling Arabic legends and parables, which were partly ancient
wisdom and partly obscenities. He had no qualms about
speaking freely in the hearing of the Arabs and was grateful
to them for giving back to him what he had lost and had
long since despaired of retrieving.

Dressed in elegant foreign clothes, easily recognizable as
such, he would go about the dim alleyways of Jerusalem and
chat with Armenian and Greek priests, drink coffee with the
owners of souvenir shops, and rent himself a room for the
night in the monastery hostels. He noticed that the Arabs
could not make up their minds as to whether he was an Israeli or a tourist, and so he took care to register in hotels under
a foreign passport, one of those that he always had on him,
and he told his Arab interlocutors that he had studied Arabic
in his youth at a European university and had already visited
Palestine in the days of the British Mandate. That innocent
trick enabled him to effect a sort of jump in time, a kind of
skipping over the days and years that he wanted to erase in
order to be close to the courtyard on the hill, at a time before
he had gone down to the settlement below, and thence to the
things that had wounded his heart, from the box of chocolates he had offered his roommates to his base treatment of
Leah. The ears now listening to his Arabic speech picked up

a voice that had died long ago; and the eyes now looking at him saw a man who had been resurrected, if only for a short time and if only to descend to the underground tunnel.

Grateful to the multitude of frightened people, to whom the sudden conquest was a puzzle, Alexander handed out money to runny-nosed children and got rid of the copper and silver jewelry, which he was compelled to buy in the shops, by pressing it into the hands of surprised peasant women, who had come from the villages to sell fruits and vegetables in the alleys. They would run after him and put clusters of grapes into his hands, showering him with blessings and kissing his hand, and he would continue walking under the arched roofs, with a cluster of grapes in his hand and awe and alarm, like one of them, in his heart.

He knew that on that very night, or in a day or two, he would go back to Tel Aviv and be a partner to the conquest that had just taken place and in deepening the humiliation that followed it, but between his wanderings around the territories and his work in Tel Aviv there lay an abyss that it had never occurred to him to bridge. He allowed these two beings to live in a state of complete separation and he had no difficulty in maintaining this division. He had long since realized that he was living in the same sort of division, except that its outline had now become stabilized and more distinct.

Who am I? It's easier for me to answer that now. What was once my private experience has now become collective experience. Formerly I was the only one out of all the children of Israel to wrestle with the Arab at his own private ford Jabok and emerge a sort of Pyrrhic victor. Now all the children of Israel are partners in this folly. Perhaps only a few know it, but they all feel it; they won and lost. They struggled and killed and slayed, and now both the victim and the victor long for each other, and there is no going back, since one of them was murdered. In fact, they were both murdered.

Generations must pass now before the dead are resurrected. Only in these few days, when I have been allowed to return—a theatrical, unreal return, in fact—to the past, I am like someone resurrected. But this is an illusion. I shall go back to being the dead man that I was, since I am a man of the past and also a man of the future—but not a man of the present. In the future many such people will walk this earth. Maybe they won't be wearing clothes bought in London; they might be wearing a tarbush, an agal, and a kaffiyeh; their mother tongue will certainly not be Russian or German. It's more likely that it will be Hebrew and Arabic. Levantines, a mingling of races, gray eyes with pitch-black hair, a race whose speech is gestures of the hand and shouts. But this thread will extend from me. I am its beginning, whether I like it or not. Meanwhile, I have received an advance on the account of the future—a few weeks in the past.

He was soon compelled to return to his work in Europe, and when he returned to Israel about a year later, the enchantment had already faded; the Arabs of the occupied territories had thrown off their initial stupefaction, threw hand grenades at the crowds of Jewish tourists in the alleys and villages, and laid mines in city centers; and the future—together with the past—had gone back to their secret hiding places, peeping in their desolation at the dusty present and allowing themselves to be recalled fleetingly by those deserving of visions—and their number was dwindling incredibly quickly.

24.

One day, the day that he became forty-one, he parked his hired car in a rain-drenched square on the outskirts of London and took a bus into town. As he dropped into the first seat he came across, he closed his eyes and fell into bleak contemplation of his birthday. The bus pulled up at the next stop, jerking him back to consciousness, and he saw two girls sitting down on the empty seat in front of him. The girl on the left had hair the color of copper—dark copper with a glint of gold. It was sleek and gathered at the nape of her neck with a black velvet ribbon, tied in a cross-shaped bow. This ribbon, like her hair, radiated a crisp freshness, a pristine freshness to be found in things as yet untouched by a fingering hand. Whoever tied that ribbon with such meticulous care? wondered Alexander. Then he waited for the moment when she would turn to her friend, and when she turned to her friend and he saw her features, his mouth fell open in a stifled cry. Or did it perhaps escape from his mouth? Anyway, the passengers did not react.

25.

From the day Alexander obtained the girl's name and address, he started sending her typewritten and unsigned letters. After a while he suggested that she write to him care of the Poste Restante in the post office in Trafalgar Square. He asked her to address the letters to Franz Kafka.

Her replies were simple, somewhat curious and surprised. Her politeness and tender age led her to reply, but her letters showed no sign of any miracle of reciprocity. She was in the last few months of her secondary school studies and Alexander would sit in the café opposite her house and watch her through the glass front. Once or twice he walked up and down along the sidewalk and positioned himself in front of her in the street, but she did not look at him. He continued to write to her from wherever he was staying and the matter went on for years. Her letters at last became what he had wanted them to be. She had clearly pictured a character for herself and was fond of this figment of her imagination. From the very first letter on, Alexander sent her records of works by Mozart and his guess proved right; she loved his music and it seemed to Alexander that the link between them had become more real and rested on a solid basis, insofar as it was possible to build a basis upon a void.

In the fourth year of their correspondence, after the girl Thea had graduated from university, it became clear to Alexander that she was going to marry an English youth by the name of G.R. Alexander had seen the youth on more than one occasion while he sat in the same café opposite Thea's home. Sometimes Alexander would sit a few tables away from them and catch snatches of their conversation. G.R. had a magnificent Lamborghini, and about a month before they were to take their marriage vows, Alexander thought of a simple idea. He introduced himself to G.R. in the café, said that he was thinking of buying himself a Lamborghini, and asked if G.R. would let him drive the car a little. G.R. willingly consented.

He was a slight youth with smooth hair that fell over his pale, smooth, girlish forehead. His hands were delicate with long fingers, his eyes were a watery blue, he dressed like a stockbroker, and his manners conformed to the letter to the etiquette taught in expensive public schools. He spoke with an Oxford accent, affected and deliberate, talked through his nose and stammered to the required extent, and there was nothing about him that could explain to Alexander why Thea was willing to become his wife. Even so he did not condemn her. Trying to interpret some sentences in her letters in an elaborate and groundless way, he believed that he himself was to blame for this step, a step in which Alexander saw a sort of despair or protest on her part because he had neither proposed nor introduced himself to her. He therefore sought to save her from herself and from the youth who would not give her happiness anyway.

After Alexander and G.R. had covered a good stretch on the highway, they went into a bar. There Alexander asked if he might take a look at the car engine, and while examining its motor he loosened several connections and left them just tight enough to allow the car to travel several hundred meters. After that they would work themselves loose and cause an accident. This was a method that had already been tested and had proved its effectiveness.

In those few seconds that Alexander was bent over the engine, several ideas passed through his mind that he had rejected until now. It was not the knowledge of G.R.'s imminent death that speeded the flood of thoughts rushing through his head: he had no pity for the lad, who was in his eyes quite stupid and in his opinion incapable of loving Thea properly. What led him to reconsider his decision to take a life was the clear and constant knowledge that he would never offer himself to her. Although he had believed for some time that the age barrier would not hinder their relationship, he knew the scenario well: As soon as it became known to the intelligence staff that he had an English mistress in London and that he was prepared to abandon his wife and home for her sake, he would be recalled at once and would not be permitted to return to work abroad. There would then be only one possibility open to him and one alone—to leave everything to Leah and the children and to leave Israel. Such a step would immediately sever all connections between him and the establishment, and even if he wanted to act as a commercial supplier in Europe, they would reject him altogether in Israel. Then he would have to resort to the one thing that he was not prepared to do—to start all over again, as his father had done when he was twenty years older than Alexander was at that time, except that Alexander did not have his father's vitality. For a long time he had lived by habit and the assets he owned. With the loss of these two, he would have nothing in his hands to offer Thea except a sort of man with a past, a kind of Polish officer from General Anders' army, with a title, living in London off the capital of a British admirer with romantic leanings and spending his days gorging himself in a club in Kensington.

If that's the case, Alexander said to himself while examining the insides of the Lamborghini, why am I killing this fool?

With fumbling fingers Alexander hurried to retighten the connections that he had just loosened; suddenly he felt weak at the knees and wanted to be as far away as possible. Now that he had made G.R. a present of his life he could no longer bear to look at his face. He told the youngster that he had to be in town straightaway, that he was late for a meeting, and that he would take a taxi.

They parted in the bar. G.R. set off toward London and the taxi arrived a quarter of an hour later. When Alexander was halfway to town in the taxi they had to stop because the road was blocked with police cars, an ambulance, and vehicles that had stopped because of an accident.

A white Lamborghini was lying crushed in a ditch, and when Alexander went up to survey the accident from a distance, he saw a pool of blood at the side of the road and on a stretcher G.R.'s body was being carried to the ambulance.

I am not guilty, said Alexander to himself. I had no hand in this. The idiot just did not know how to drive. He was zooming into town like a lunatic. Thea was waiting for him and his head was giddy with love.

26.

Thea was appointed to teach Spanish literature at a university in Kent. After G.R.'s death her letters to Alexander took an emotional and endearing tone, and if he had wanted—and he did want very much—he could have found signs of longing in them. Thea and Alexander were now standing in the very same place, in that ethereal plain where only souls come into contact with each other, separate from the body and having no ties to it. At least it was like that for her. And Alexander would kiss her letters and close his eyes.

He went to Kent, took a room in a hotel, and would wander along the road around the university. One day he saw Thea walking alone in an elm grove.

After that he traveled to Madrid on business, and there, as he sat in a café waiting for an agent to meet him, two shots were fired at him and both of them hit him. He was taken to hospital; from there they transferred him to Israel, and after several months he recovered. Since his cover had been blown, there was no longer any point in his working abroad, but he claimed that it would be stupid for them to do without his experience and his many connections. So he suggested that he undergo plastic surgery on his face, but his superiors categorically refused.

So it was clear that he would not be going to Europe anymore and that as far as his work was concerned he would be finally grounded. He was required to sign a document that stipulated that if he ever wanted to make a private trip abroad he would have to grow a mustache and beard.

Now he lied to Thea and wrote,

> I haven't written to you for ten months. . . . Ten
> months ago they fired two shots at me and both of them
> hit me. . . . We have good doctors and they stitched me
> up, but from a professional point of view my cover had
> been blown. . . . And so that I would be able to carry

on with my work I had to undergo a further operation that deprived me of my original face forever. . . . I am now able to comply with your request of several years ago. The photograph in this envelope is of my face as it was until a year ago.

On the last day of the month I shall be in your home town and you can send me a letter care of the post office. You will be in your provincial town at the university, as agreed, at 1700 hours.

He telephoned a friend in London and asked him to pick up the letter in Trafalgar Square and to send it to Tel Aviv. In her reply Thea wrote:

My darling, you are perhaps, after all, my only darling.

After seven years you show me your face, which is no longer your face. Have you ever thought, sanely, as other people think, about what you are inflicting on me? . . .

And now you have another face, but I am sure that they have not touched your eyes—you didn't let them damage your eyes—and I shall recognize you by those eyes. Please walk past me in the street again, as you say you have done many times before. You'll see that I shall stop you in the street, and so that you'll be convinced that I really have recognized you without a shadow of doubt, I shall fall into your arms without warning. . . .

Like a leopard's prey, I am yours,
Thea

He read through her letter again and again and for the first time considered the possibility that they might meet, and thus the last card would be laid on the table, and with the final victory, as far as was possible to tell, would also come the final blow. There was no doubt in his heart that Thea was ready to fall into his arms, but he also knew that he would have nothing to offer her apart from the initial giddiness. In the dance—which he was ready to join—he would be tottering to his end.

When he was ready to meet the angel and be crushed by its final and deadly embrace, something unlucky happened to him. Wearing his new mustache and beard, he went to Europe; during the passport control, he made a mistake for the first time in his life and presented—out of the three passports in his possession—the wrong one. He was taken for questioning, he had a body search, and they found his loaded revolver. He was immediately taken into custody.

27.

As he sat in prison he waited patiently for the trial and for his deportation from England. Henceforth all his thoughts centered on the meeting with Thea. He knew that he would have no difficulty in returning to England via another country, on another passport, and with his beard and mustache clipped shorter or allowed to grow longer. The months he spent in prison were the happiest of his life.

Thea, who had been stunned by several comments in his last letter, wrote to him:

> Forgive me if I have made a mistake. Forgive me for the terrible thing I am about to write. I only want to ask. You yourself drove me to this question.
>
> I have not stopped thinking about the compliments you pay me on my detective abilities. You praise the way I explained the expression in your eyes, and at the same time you write that luckily for you I did not draw "far-reaching conclusions."
>
> Tell me, and please be honest, because I have always believed your every word, tell me, did you have a hand in the death of G.R.?
>
> > Thea

Alexander, who never received this letter, could not write from prison either; and when much more time had elapsed and Thea did not receive any news from him, she went on to write:

> Unhappy man, my poor tortured man,
> I'd be willing never to send the letter I put in the box, if only you would write. Nearly six months have gone

by. Why do you remain silent? Please don't die, I beg
you. Let me into your secret; I might want to go with
you. I might want to leave you and tear up your letters.
You can't treat me like this. I am not an office. I am a
woman approaching her twenty-sixth year. Why do you
demand so much of me?

I do not doubt your love, but I am not equal to love
like this. It is as if I am your widow. You have no right
to die and you have no right to remain silent. Tell me
what I am to do.

This letter never reached him either, and when at last he
came out of prison and was deported to his country, he decided that this time he would prepare everything he needed
for the final journey and would not write to Thea until the
day when he stood in front of her. Just before this event he
would shave off his beard and mustache.

About a month after this he flew back to England in a
plane from Dublin and immediately contacted one of his
former subordinates in London. He brought with him everything he had managed to amass from his bank account and
from the sale of shares, and since he knew that he would
never go back home, he was free from the worries of his previous work. He made up a plausible story for his subordinate
and asked him to help by collecting all the data available on
a certain Miss Thea B., who taught Spanish at the university
in Kent. After about two weeks he received the following report:

The beauty in question lives in Residence Number Six,
Room Fourteen. Until a short while ago she lived on her
own, well liked by the staff and a good teacher. About a
month ago a whirlwind romance developed between her
and a visiting lecturer from Madrid. His name is Dr. Nikos Trianda. The general impression is that they are
both head over heels in love. The visitor from Madrid is
about thirty-eight, good-looking; your teacher has well-off
parents in London. I wish you success, Alex, if you are
looking for something like that in her, but it looks as if
you have turned up at the wrong time.

Alexander went on to Kent, and since he already knew the campus, he went that very day to the office and asked to see Dr. Nikos Trianda. He was told that the man was not staying on campus. Alexander was given a telephone number and he rang from the university office and asked to meet him for lunch the following day in a restaurant in the center of the village. He said that he was interested in a research grant from the University of Madrid.

On leaving the office he saw Thea in the corridor. She was talking to two students—a man and a woman—with a file under her arm and her face turned to him in profile. Alexander hurried out into the courtyard and from there he went to the hotel.

> I am not changing anything of the decision which I made [he recorded in his diary]. I have burned all my bridges behind me, the way ahead is wide open, and I shall go along it. I knew several months of happiness in prison and eight years of another kind of happiness stretch out behind me. Now I shall pay the price of pleasure. Nikos Trianda is, almost beyond doubt, the name of that Greek who came before me about twelve years ago. I would have been able to shoot him then, not now. If I had tightened the screws in G.R.'s Lamborghini properly, I would have found Thea divorced by now and perhaps no less prepared to follow me— and perhaps more so—than she was, in my imagination, about a month ago. Tomorrow I shall see Trianda, but I have no designs on him. Tricks of that sort work once, not twice, especially if they fail when they succeed, or when they do not succeed. The circle is well and truly closed, and Alexander Abramov is fucked up.

28.

As he went into the restaurant, having arrived about ten minutes early and lain in wait for Nikos around the corner so as to take a look at him, he was certain that the man in front of him was the man whom he had interrogated on the subject of his links with a Greek priest in the Old City of Jerusalem.

Alexander introduced himself as Gyorg Milan, apologized for troubling Mr. Trianda during his sabbatical, and explained that he had heard from acquaintances about a lecturer from the University of Madrid and could not resist asking for a short interview.

Gyorg Milan told him that he was trying to finish a research project on the ancient Phoenician trade routes and was wondering if there was any possibility of getting a grant in Madrid, since he would have to spend about six months in Spain and on the North African coast.

Nikos Trianda looked at Mr. Milan's face with great curiosity and this did not escape Alexander's notice. Trianda, however, did not recognize him, and with great enthusiasm he said that the subject was very dear to his heart and that he himself, although he was not an expert in matters of economics, dealt with that wonderful, marvelous sphere that went by the name of the Mediterranean.

From then on, Alexander listened for a long time to what he had longed to hear from Trianda a dozen years before, and now he had no interest whatsoever in it. He saw before him a pleasant, cheerful, and likable man, full of intellectual curiosity and in an elated mood. Alexander did not take his eyes off the man and once more said to himself that he would have been able to shoot him dead years ago, but that now he had no intention of doing so. All the same he suggested that it would be worth their while, meeting again, even if there were no prospect of getting a grant in Madrid, since they had so many common interests to talk about. Perhaps Dr. Trianda would agree to meet him again the following day? He had a comfortable car and they would be able to go to one of the nearby beaches in the afternoon—and even though it was not a beach of the Mediterranean, so dear to them both, it was at least the seashore; they could use their imagination, and they could sit there in some little pub and chat awhile.

Trianda said that it would be a pleasure for him to do so, but the academic year was drawing to a close and in a few days he would be leaving here for good; in fact, he went on and laughed, he would be leaving in the company of someone who might change the whole course of his life. Mr. Milan, as a man, would no doubt understand and would not be angry that he had regretfully to decline the invitation. No doubt they would meet again, if—in spite of the meagerness of the university's funds—Mr. Milan reached Spain under his own steam. "Here is my card," said Trianda. "I shall be delighted if you get in touch."

With this they parted. In the evening Nikos mentioned to Thea that he had met a man who had a dream similar to his own and that even in his outward appearance there was something of the ancient charm of the Mediterranean; he had an Assyrian beard and was built like Hercules. Thea said that she had apparently seen the man in the corridor of the university. She had noticed his build and his beard, but she had not thought that he was Hercules, because as he left the corridor he stumbled and almost tripped in the doorway. Thea had thought that the man was very old.

Alexander returned to London, and on the day that Thea and Nikos arrived he saw them getting out of a car and going into her parents' house. Alexander himself was sitting in his regular place in the café opposite her parents' house, below the flat of the late G.R.

For three days running he sat there. During the afternoon the windows of Thea's flat were open and through the window frame he saw her mother a few times, moving about the living room, around the dining table, as far as one could see. He saw Thea and Nikos every day at least twice, leaving the building arm in arm. Once he tried to follow them at a distance, afraid that Nikos would notice him, but his attempt was in vain. They stopped a taxi and went off in it. They came back about three hours later with parcels and shopping bags in their hands. Alexander saw how Thea, in the doorway of the building, raised her face to Nikos, stood on tiptoe, and kissed him on the mouth, and then they went in.

He had a revolver in his pocket, a loaded revolver with a silencer. As he sat at his table in the café, less than a stone's throw from the passersby in the street, whose clothes brushed the glass front as they went past, he would sip from the cup in front of him and let his thoughts wander. He remembered what Chekhov said about loaded revolvers: "If a revolver appears in the first act of a play it must be fired in the third act." Well, I have news for you, my dear Anton Pavlovitch, said

Alexander. A revolver can appear in the first act and be fired pointlessly, and despite this it will be a play worth performing, a tragicomedy, perfect in all respects and worthy of the pen of any adept writer.

When he had exhausted all these thoughts and did not have the energy to concoct new ones, he went back to himself and Thea. It occurred to him that the time had come to write a last letter to her before they met face to face—perhaps that very day, at the latest in two days' time—before Nikos took her beyond retrieval. They needed a document that would set a seal on the whole affair, for she still knew him only through the letters, and before she saw him with her own eyes, because then—after they met for the first time—they might never meet again. Perhaps he would also write to Leah and the children, but he would do that later. First he would write to Thea.

> I bear no grudge against you in my heart, and we are at last about to meet now, and perhaps you will be mine, and mine alone, infinitely more than you ever were poor G.R.'s or more than you will ever belong to cheerful Trianda. I know that we shall meet and the hour is not far away. You have never sinned against me, not once, my terrible and wonderful angel. It is I alone who have brought about this abominable state of affairs in which we find ourselves. I was hesitant, tried to have it my way, a coward, a miserable and despicable coward. Someone who was privileged to know of your existence before he met you, should have been with you all the days of his life, with you alone. But I rested on the way, I stopped off, I left signs, I murdered a woman whom fate placed next to me on the school bench when she was six; I begot a son who will soon perhaps celebrate my death, and two girls who hope that I never come back to disturb their orphaned state. In the file of the secret agent Alexander Abramov it will be recorded that his end bore witness to his beginning—complete failure, almost betrayal. In the house on the hill, when the news of my end reaches them, Leah will rummage through the drawers and find scraps of a diary that she will read and she will not know what she is reading; then she will

go to the cardboard box in the bottom of the wardrobe and bring out of its hiding place the petticoat she has kept for nineteen years now and she will find in its folds the herbs she collected in the orchard, and she will clasp my mother's lace petticoat to her heart and will believe that she is united with other days, days of young love, and will not know that she has no portion in the closed circle that Ingeborg, Abram, and Alexander Abramov drew around themselves in order to protect themselves from the world. They protected themselves until the end and each one of them died a dog's death, as lonely as a star no telescope has discovered and therefore no one ever wants to reach.

But you and I, Thea, we have been—despite it all we have already been—beyond this horror, because we met in the inner circle that I drew for myself when I was a child, when I was driven away from home and looked for a way to return. In that third circle, within the very heart of the music, in the presence of the true and only son of God, we were immersed together, burning in the light. That was a light no orgasm has the power to kindle; we were united in a love whose power was greater than that with which people love themselves.

It grieves me that I shall never know what a man feels when he comes out of this circle and finds you at his side. I can only guess: When he looks into your eyes and touches the skin of your face with his fingers, it is impossible for him not to feel that there is a way to return to the inner circle, a way in which he can go back in and out of it until the day of his death. And then perhaps to remain inside it forever. And perhaps not alone. It's possible to believe it, when you're with me, Thea. Indeed you are with me. It cannot be denied.

29.

On the third day of his vigil opposite Thea's parents' home, the man who had fired two shots at him in Madrid, a year before, came into the café. He knew that he would find him there; in his hands was a photograph of Alexander with his beard and mustache.

The man walked up to his table and shot at him.

Thea, her parents, and Nikos were sitting at tea in the drawing room. They heard the sound of a shot, put down their teacups, got up, and looked out of the window.

The first shot hit Alexander in the chest and ripped his lungs. He lifted up his head to draw breath and opened his mouth. Time stood still. Alexander saw himself from the side and he was a gladiator, mortally wounded in the arena, and as if by witchcraft he began to change slowly until he turned into a large, dumb beast with a huge head, the head of a bull or stag, but a man from the shoulders down. Then, as in the etching by Picasso from *Vollard Suite* that hung on the wall of his childhood room, Alexander saw Thea leaning from the gallery trying to touch his dying head.

In that split second, when time stood still, he saw Thea standing in the window and her hand was floating in the air, passing slowly over the street, above the hooting cars and above the frightened people who had gathered there at the sound of the shot; and her white hand, its five fingers spread out like the wings of a dove—one of the doves that he used to bring alive to the Arab cook—floated through the air, coming closer and closer, and soon it would touch his forehead and they would be one.

Then the second shot was fired and it split his forehead open at the spot the white transparent hand was about to touch. Alexander asked her forgiveness for not having managed to hold out a little longer.

An ambulance forced its way down the street and stopped in front of the café door. The driver and his assistant took a stretcher from the ambulance and went inside with it. They soon came out carrying a covered body.

The next day Thea saw the picture in the newspapers and Nikos also saw it. He urged her to go on living, demanded the pills that she had bought from the chemist. Thea asked him to go to Madrid and not to come until she called him; he was forced to comply but insisted on his right to phone every day.

Her father answered the first phone call that same night

and said that she was well. She had already been asleep in bed for several hours. When he phoned the following day, he listened for a long time to the ringing at the other end, but nobody came to answer the call.

Yarnton, 1979

**A HAUNTING LOVE STORY, A RICH
EVOCATIVE NOVEL OF AN ISRAELI
FAMILY THROUGH FOUR GENERATIONS
OF CONFLICT AND ENDURANCE**

REQUIEM FOR NA'AMAN

A NOVEL BY
BENJAMIN TAMMUZ
AUTHOR OF
MINOTAUR

**AN ORIGINAL HARDCOVER NOVEL
FROM NAL BOOKS
MAY, 1982 RELEASE**

❧ 1. ❧

AMONG those who commit suicide, the fortunate ones come by paper and pencil at their side at the decisive moment, and they write to us and explain to us; and although we will never make peace or agree with this, nevertheless the circle has somehow been closed and one can say that there has been no neglect or omission. But the unfortunate suicides are those who become so confused in their minds that instead of writing to us they speak to themselves, imagining that their words reach us, for we are, after all, their dear ones. Though it is not in malice that they do so, in the end the link connecting the dead with the living will be missing; and without this link—precarious as it may be—whence will culture grow?

❧ 2. ❧

THERE was a woman in our settlement, during the Nineties of the previous century, named Bella-Yaffa,* and her husband's name was Froyke-Ephraim† and they had a son and a

---

* *Bella* and *Yaffa* both mean "beautiful."
† *Froyke* is the Russian-Yiddish diminutive for the Hebrew *Ephraim*.

daughter, Na'aman and Sarah, and seventeen acres of cereal crops and six acres of almond trees and vines with a house, a stable, and a cow shed, and in the yard there were pigeons and chickens and kitchen vegetables planted behind the cow shed.

At night the moon pours its greenish light upon the yard, and the scraps of iron and wood scattered about move and whirl like living creatures, and the woman Bella-Yaffa leans on the porch rail, and is silent, and her husband works in the kitchen, and he too is silent, from experience; and some time later he comes out and places a hand on his wife's shoulder, to lead her to the bedroom, and then the woman says, "Look, Froyke, what magic there is all around us, what dreadful sadness."

And the husband says, "Bella, what, what will become of the children?"

3.

AT the end of that year, in the autumn, about a week before the High Holy Days, when the husband went to the Council House to examine accounts, Bella-Yaffa placed a saddle on the white stallion and rode out of the settlement. Schoolchildren later related that they had seen her riding toward the wadi.

In the early evening she crossed the plain of Sharon and rode north all night. Before dawn she reached a hilly place with wadis, and there she tied the stallion to a hedge of acacia trees and continued on foot toward cover at the foot of the hill. When the sky began to clear Bella-Yaffa saw through the heaps of stones, several trees and a rocky slope closing the horizon. She made an effort to remember the names of the trees but could not. Then from her bag she took the bottle she had brought with her and drew out the cork.

ᘯᘓᕢ 4. ᕢᘓ

AND these are the words the woman spoke to her husband and children:

"I try to remember when the beginning was. Maybe when I was five or six, when my father took me by cart to a wedding in a neighboring village. We left the city in the morning and for the first time in my life I saw open spaces, fields the color of gold, and avenues of slender trees, their trunks white with black stains, slender trees running like naked ghosts into infinity. I burst out crying and my father took me in his arms and hid my face inside his coat and whispered to me, 'Don't look at this defilement, Bella. It's a false charm, a vanity of the Gentiles. One of these days we'll get out of here and go to the land of our fathers. . . . There you'll see real trees, cedars of Lebanon. . . . The Redemption is not far off. . . . Another year or two, with God's grace, and our feet will tread on the soil of the destroyed sanctuary. . . .'

"When we returned from the wedding I had a fierce yearning to come back to those fields again, to run with the slender trees, the trembling and fluttering birches, and to vanish, together with them, into those terrible expanses my father had cursed. And at the same time I understood that if I really were to run with the trees, I would myself reach those mountains of cedars, without having to wait a year or two, which seemed to me like eternity. . . . Froyke, my dear, you brought me to the land of my father's dreams and I am requiting you with evil for good. . . . Why did you never ask me why I mixed poison in the cup of salvation? Why did you love me, despite my being so evil? If you had asked, if you had had the desire to hear, I would have told you. . . . You are so happy, toiling in the fields and vineyards, rejoicing in your children, forgiving a wife who walks around your house like a ghost, in the house in which you serve as both father and mother, to both me and the children together. . . . And I, where am I going? That first revelation, riding with my father in the cart, was the first and the last. Add to it the songs which my ears absorbed in that country. . . . Add to it the names of the flowers and the trees, which I knew and whispered in my sleep. . . . Where are those cedars, Froyke? Now, beside this ruin, I see trees I don't know, and I will never know their names. . . . It may be that our forefathers, the ancient men of the desert, knew their names—but I don't know them. It's impossible to know things that came to an end thousands of years ago. It's possible to love only what has grown close to your bare feet, in the dawn of your childhood, Froyke. I suspect that you're lying, Froyke, when you seem to love this wilderness. . . . But how can I say that to you, when you look so happy, strong, pouring the sweat of your brow on the ominous rocks around the small and alien house you built with your own hands, a house without a thatched roof or a clay oven, without a chimney. . . .

"Forgive me, Froyke, my heart burns with a yearning for the place my father cursed so vigorously. . . . Had you spoken to me and asked me, I might have told you that the destroyed sanctuary, the dream my father left me, may perhaps become our children's lot. . . . As for me, my soul longs for the dream, but I sense that it dwells beyond the place to which those birches ran like mad, and I also am going there, perhaps in order to be with you and the children at last . . . to be truly, wholeheartedly, forever. Froyke, my love, I love the dream more than I love you. . . . I am a soul struck off from the book of life. Remember me, Froyke, kiss the children. . . . They're little, they'll forget me."

5.

THE woman drew the cork from the bottle and for a moment a sour and moldy smell rose to her nostrils, like the smell hovering about the shed at the back of the yard when Froyke-Ephraim soaks the almond-shells in water, as fodder for the cattle. For a moment the woman seemed to have gone back on her decision, but then she quickly lifted the bottle to her lips and drank the liquid to the last drop. She lay down on her back and from the corner of her eye saw the sun rising over the slope. Then fierce pains attacked her in her stomach, and through gritted teeth she emitted some shouts mingled with words in a foreign language. An old vineyard watchman, an Arab from a nearby village, heard her cries and drew near to where she lay. He leaned over the woman, who was now whispering and sobbing, and a sour smell rose to his nose. He had never seen a Jewish woman drunk, and the thing was a wonder in his eyes. At first he tried to revive her by waving his hand, to bring some of the morning breeze to her nostrils, but when he saw her closing her eyes and falling asleep, illicit thoughts came to him. Bella-Yaffa was twenty-five years old when she died, with a perfect beauty, as her husband would remember to his dying day.

When the old Arab realized that the woman was dead, he dragged some stones of the place and covered her corpse, until the pile could not be distinguished from all the other heaps of rubble all around.

✣ 6. ✣

WHEN Froyke-Ephraim came back from the Council House and found the children crying, he made them a meal and went to the cow shed and from there to the stable. And in the stable he found that the white stallion was gone. Only in the evening did he hear from the schoolchildren that they had seen the woman riding toward the wadi. Immediately the man set out in the same direction, on a borrowed horse. Two neighbors rode out too, one to the west, to the seashore, and the other to the east, to the hills. All three returned toward morning, exhausted and stunned. That day they sent messengers to the Jewish settlements in Judea, Samaria, and Galilee, where they bribed Turkish gendarmes to keep their eyes and ears open and report back about what they saw and heard, and they also sent a letter to the newspaper *Ha-Levanon* in Jerusalem, asking the editors to print a notice to the public about the woman whose traces had vanished.

The High Holy Days came and went, the first rains descended and the earth was plowed in readiness for the sowing. After Passover Froyke-Ephraim reaped his field and bound his sheaves and at the beginning of the summer journeyed to the Chief Rabbi to ask him for permission to take another wife, the widow of a farmer killed some six months earlier. The Chief Rabbi was hesitant, and said that according to the strict rule of justice the law permitted it, but that according to the merciful approach to justice it would be proper to wait.

Upon hearing this Froyke-Ephraim became enraged and shouted, "Leave the merciful approach to justice to me, Honored Rabbi. My heart is broken as it is."

And Froyke-Ephraim found himself another rabbi, in Jaffa, who agreed to conduct the wedding immediately after Bella-Yaffa was declared divorced.

The widow, a strong and merry woman named Rivka, brought him as dowry a five-year-old boy, named Aminadav, seventeen acres of cereal crops, six acres of vines and almond trees, a house with a piano and also a cow shed, but no stable. Rivka had sold the pair of horses after her husband's death to maintain herself and her son Aminadav. And since Froyke-Ephraim's white stallion had also been lost, as is known, one letter was sent to Paris, to Baron Rothschild, and another letter to Odessa, to the Council which supported Jewish settlement in the Land of Israel, both letters containing thorough explanations that allotments of thirty-four acres of cereal crops could not be worked without horses.

The Baron and the Council in Odessa replied as they replied.

In time Na'aman, Froyke-Ephraim's first son from his first marriage, began to strike upon the piano which his stepmother had brought to the house.

❧ 7. ❧

AFTER Froyke-Ephraim brought the woman Rivka to his house, the Council of the settlement convened an extraordinary session, and there tempers flared up violently. In particular their anger turned against the Jaffa rabbi who had permitted the marriage. They called him a hypocrite, for only some six months earlier he had forbidden the staging of a theatrical performance by Jews in Jaffa, because he had found arguments in the Gemarah* that theaters were idolatry. That being so, whence had he the authority to permit an immediate marriage between a widow and a man whose wife had vanished without trace?

If the truth be told, the farmers had never liked Bella-Yaffa. It can be said that they had hated her in their hearts. But people fight for a principle more than they give themselves over to the love of others, because a principle is hatred of the opponent.

But before the vote was taken it was decided to invite Froyke-Ephraim to the meeting, so that he could say what he had to say in his defense.

And these are the words that Froyke-Ephraim spoke in their presence:

"Gentlemen and my brother farmers, first of all let me inform you that I am speaking on behalf of two plots of cereal crops and two plots of vines and almond trees, from which the intelligent will easily grasp that I have two votes in any count. And secondly, consider that it was not for the love of women or the lust of the flesh that I brought a new wife into my house. Only the redemption of the land lay before my eyes, and how can I bear to see the fields turn fallow and desolate because I don't have a woman in the house to give a hand with raising the children, milking the cows, and doing the kitchen work? My brother farmers, was it not to work the land that we came to the land of our fathers? Is not working the land considered equal to worshiping the Creator? And who am I to dispute the decision of the rabbi from Jaffa? I am a farmer, a tiller of the soil, not a sage learned in the Torah. Please, my friends, consider this and do not betray our common goal, the exalted aim of regenerating the wastes of the Land of Israel and of restoring the dispersions of our people, to bring them back to our land, a land flowing with milk and honey. And God who dwells on

---

* The second, concluding section of the Talmud, supplying a commentary on the first part, the Mishnah.

high, He shall look down upon us from His height of heights, and He will judge, for it is for Him to judge and for us to do the work."

Thus spoke Froyke-Ephraim on that day, and the farmers listened and remained silent a long while. Finally they gave up the vote and it was decided that if one day a master in the Torah happened to come to the settlement, they would place the matter before him. And on his part Froyke-Ephraim promised that if Bella-Yaffa, the woman who had vanished, were found, he would restore her honorably to her place in his house, and would also adopt the second woman, Rivka, into his household, as the rabbi would decree, without depriving her, God forbid, of her share in the fields and vineyards which she had brought him as a dowry.

And life returned to normal and the present was not distinguishable from the past. Only he who sees into the heart knows that Froyke-Ephraim did not forget Bella-Yaffa, and at night he saw her in his dreams and spoke to her words of entreaty and love.

ᘐᘏᕙ 8. ᕉᘎᘐ

ABOUT a year and a half after these events, the First Zionist Congress took place in the city of Basel, in Switzerland, and there appeared the man whom many saw as the king of the Jews, in other words, Doctor Benjamin Ze'ev Theodor Herzl. And when a male child was born to Froyke-Ephraim and Rivka, they named him Herzl, and on the day that they celebrated his circumcision, Froyke-Ephraim make a speech. The Secretary of the Council wrote down the speaker's words, and they are recorded in the register of the settlement, and if it has not been eaten by moths, or burned in fires, and if its pages were not scattered in the pogroms that the Arabs wrought upon the settlement, and if it did not rot in the rains when the Turks refused the settlers permission to put a roof on the new Council House which they had built without a permit, then his words are still inscribed there for generations to come, in eternal remembrance.

Such was the surface of things, stormy on the outside. But

within, the streams of life flowed serenely and tranquilly, as befitted the lives of settlers. The changes took place according to the seasons of the year and shifting agricultural requirements, and if something happened that digressed from this cycle, the farmers were startled to see that not one year had passed, but seven or ten. And a man would say to his neighbor: Look, ha!—and I didn't know.

...om the author of the brilliant, highly acclaimed *Minotaur*, an intricate, lyrical novel about an Israeli family through four generations . . .

REQUIEM FOR NA'AMAN

A NOVEL BY
BENJAMIN TAMMUZ

AUTHOR OF
MINOTAUR

Set against eighty years of peace and war, striving and struggle, this is the haunting story of a family, a people, and of the conflict between love and duty. A metaphor for the birth of Israel, and, ultimately, a telling commentary on the human condition, *Requiem for Na'aman* pictures as never before the meaning and cost of Israel's endurance.

An original hardcover novel
from NAL Books
#H417—$12.95 U.S., $14.95 Canada